THE

HAUNTED

GHOST

AAYUSH DAS

Become

.com

First published in 2018 by

Becomeshakespeare.com

Wordit Content Design & Editing Services Pvt Ltd
Unit - 26, Building A -1, Nr Wadala RTO,
Wadala (East), Mumbai 400037, India
T: +91 8080226699

Wordit Art Fund helps deserving authors publish their work by providing monetary support. To apply for funding, please visit us at www.BecomeShakespeare.com

Cover Illustration Copyright © 2017 by Aayush Das

Editing by Aayush Das

Author Photograph by Ayush Thakur

ISBN - 978-93-87649-30-9

Dedicated to dad. You may be lost to me, but you will always be in my memories.

About the Author

Since 1994, the Author has been an undercover member of the fabled Illuminati. He's a skilled master of deception and disguise. He has a day job, he goes to the gym for about twenty days in one calendar year, and he lives in the most inconspicuous country on the planet. The perfect disguise. He lurks in the shadows and secretly works towards his evil agenda of world domination. Like most cunning villains of legend, he is narcissistic. He writes in his free time, stories and novels about the most unworldly things. Like a true escapist, he is lazy and rarely finishes the books that he starts writing. Top secret intelligence reports say that he unwittingly leaves clues about his grand evil plans in his stories and books, but he remains unfazed. In the 21st century world where tons of information flows in all directions all the time, his work may just pass as white noise in the background. The odds against humanity are high. The future looks bleak. Will some hero or heroine step up and shoulder the tumultuous task of reading his mind-numbingly boring work? If at all that happens, humanity just might stand a chance against the evil Author.

Contents

Prologue

Adalwulf tripped, again. Protruding roots this time, perhaps. The two men couldn't see much in the dark, and they had no time to hazard guesses. Their lives were in danger. Fifty souls. Men, women, children. They had just watched their entire cult being murdered. Shred to pieces by that thing. He had warned Dorcha. They had all warned Dorcha. Alchemy was a progressive science, but there were rules that ought not to be broken. Not even in Alchemy.

They took shelter under the waterfall. Dorcha produced muffled screams of pain, holding a rag between his teeth. Another rag was pressed hard against his bloodied abdomen. He had lived, perhaps, because she wasn't aware of her own strength when she attacked him. A screaming Dorcha ran out of the house, and fainted. Perhaps she thought he was dead. She quickly started snapping necks and removing heads off of the villagers. Meanwhile, Adalwulf picked him up and ran away.

But they knew nobody else survived.

Dorcha coughed up some more blood, breathing in spurts.

"What have you done?" Adalwulf looked into his blank, green eyes.

"You know," Dorcha said. "You know exactly what I have done."

Europe. Thirteenth century BC. Alchemy, a science that attempted to achieve perfection, was becoming popular amongst secret cults. Villages sufficiently isolated from the larger part of the world were perfect for such cults to use. One such village, Neoma, was home to the greatest Alchemist of all time - Dorcha Piper. The young Alchemist was the man who had researched and contemplated the idea of immortality like nobody in his time could. Twelve years. In that time he invented many concoctions and potions that could exorcise evil spirits without harming the human host. And this young Alchemist was the man who had just perfected immortality. And he did it on his wife.

"How did you do all this?" Adalwulf asked. "How did you turn Marcia into *that*?"

"It's a matter of principle," Dorcha whispered faintly. "All this time Alchemy has been about purifying elements and creating the perfect element, a Philosopher's Stone. But I don't think that the key to immortality is an *element*."

"What do you mean to say?"

"Think about it. God made *us* in his own image, so that we could rule this world. God creates perfection, and only God knows how to achieve it. If there is a cure to mortality, it cannot be an element of our making. No. It has to be an element fashioned by God. The essence of life is the answer to death."

"Blood," Adalwulf gasped.

"Yes, blood. But the cult would not have it. They would brand me a heretic, destroy me and my methods. I could never let that happen."

Dorcha coughed again. Adalwulf steadied his friend and shook him. Dorcha could not be allowed to sleep. In the state they were in, it would mean certain death.

"So you used blood for the ritual," Adalwulf said. "But what did you really do?"

"You cannot possibly think that I will tell you," Dorcha cried. "That thing I created, that is not Alchemy. That is not perfection. It is something else entirely."

Adalwulf thought about trying to convince his friend some more, but Dorcha was unwavering in his resolve. What he had done that night was a secret that could never be divulged.

"I have to find a way. I have to undo the unholy abomination that I have made."

"Listen, friend," Adalwulf stopped him. "There is nothing unholy here. You said it yourself. Blood is the essence of life. The true Philosopher's Stone. Blood is the answer to the question of mortality. What you made tonight is a being that feeds on blood. It takes life to further its own. Is it not how Alchemy always has been? To create something new, something of equal value must be lost. We need to study more before we jump to any conclusions."

"Study what Adalwulf?" Dorcha's voice was faint as a whisper now. "Study what? That thing out there? That thing, which annihilated our village and murdered every living soul it encountered? God, what has she become?"

Adalwulf could not think of an answer. He was as shaken up as his friend.

"But why Marcia?" he asked. "Why did you do that ritual on your wife? You hated her. It makes no sense."

"I did not mean to immortalise her," Dorcha was frantic. "The first experiment is always supposed to end in failure. The first test subject is always supposed to die. *She* was supposed to die. I wanted to kill her, and use the knowledge I gained from the experiment to further my research. And then...and then…"

"You wanted to become immortal yourself," Adalwulf helped him state the obvious.

"Yes, I...that is what I wanted."

"That means we are both going to die tonight," Adalwulf said, "because you were much better at your job than you expected."

"What do you mean we are both going to die?"

Adalwulf stood up, laughing hysterically.

"You are such a fool, Dorcha. You created an immortal being that consumes blood. And you were bleeding all the way from the village to this place. Marcia wanted us to get away. She designed this cat and mouse game with you. She is just toying with her food. She will be here any minute to…"

A dull, loud crack echoed through the cavern. Loud enough to be heard over the drizzling of the waterfall.

"Wrong," a deep, feminine voice rang. Dorcha froze in his spot, unable to even draw breath. He looked straight ahead, his eyes fixated at the moonlit waterfall. It was total darkness, but an image of two glowing red eyes reflected off the watery curtain. A pair of cold hands slowly slithered down his shoulders.

"I am already here!"

Work...As Usual

"It has been a while since something interesting happened in the mortal world," said Saurush, his eyes ambling through the hefty ledgers. It didn't stir any reaction anywhere around him, only the sound of pages being turned followed his voice. His desk had recently been moved to the middle cubicle, five workspaces away from Aadesh. Apparently their chattiness during work had been distracting the other accountants.

Of course, Saurush knew it was all bullcrap. The whole obsession with workplace ethics was a cover. It was just a ploy to make the accountants a little more miserable. He knew it, he always had. The bureaucracy had always been corrupt and sadistic towards the common accountant. The enforcers bullied them and the officers did everything possible to make their job uncomfortable. Things were still better in the south where things had a proper system and the comfort and happiness of the accountants was given first priority. Aadesh had told him that all the fronts in the south were uninhabited islands or sparsely populated seafronts with great natural view and peaceful ambience to work in. In the east the fronts were more similar to the Delhi front, but it was still a corporate office environment and the management had spent big bucks on noise-cancellation magic.

Those facilities could never be used in the Delhi front. The officers would get the paperwork stuck in some department or the other. One year legal got "suspicious" about the "exorbitant" prices that the witches had quoted, the other time it was finance which couldn't release funds because the bills weren't "itemised enough". Even mortals weren't so blatant in their scandals. "Maybe because they die after a while, and the new guy has to learn the tricks of the trade from scratch," was Saurush's opinion on the matter. "In our case, there is no new guy ever. Just us. And we have no means of entertainment besides watching the mortal realm grind at a snail's pace."

"Stop it," Aadesh said, his voice sounding deeper than usual. "It is annoying."

"You bet it is. We deserve either better pay or better perks."

"I'm not talking about perks or pay." Aadesh wouldn't look up from his ledger. "I'm talking about you and your annoying habit of speaking of the 'mortal world' as if it is some other dimension."

"Well but it is another dimension," Saurush said. "We might share the same infrastructure, but make no mistake. It is a whole different level of quackery."

"Right now the only quack in this room is you."

"If you knew that little runt over there, you wouldn't be saying what you are saying." He pointed towards the creature who was sitting next to Aadesh, a creature who made an unbelievable amount of noise for someone her size.

Aadesh turned to look at the girl, who was busy contorting her face to react to something one of her peers had said to her. "I can't believe you spend time observing these...slow things."

"They're not slow." Saurush chimed in. "They just experience time differently. You would know if you had any idea where you came from."

Aadesh sat up straighter.

"Oh, how stupid of me," Saurush said. "You made the enforcer's choice. I keep forgetting that. Too many memories in this old head."

Aadesh had slipped back into his ledger. "I do not have time to respond to you. I want to finish this page before the commotion begins."

Speak of the devil. No sooner than the words had left his mouth, a loud bell went off marking the beginning of three hours of distraction.

"Whoops, seems your page shall remain unfinished."

Aadesh buried his face in his hands. "You were stalling. On purpose. You knew their session was about to start."

Saurush pointed to an obscure spot outside the window. "Your pal has been here for fifteen minutes now. He is quite the alarm clock, if you can spot him."

Aadesh turned. It was hard to see much in the fog, but his eyes were trained to scour all kinds of terrains to spot enemies. He was right there under the shed of the bicycle stand across the playground, standing perfectly still. He was wearing the white hooded robe, the standard camouflage pattern for foggy days, but Aadesh could spot the blue cuff stripes from miles away. He once used to salute to those blue cuff stripes. "The Captain, why does he keep coming here?"

"He wants you back on your previous job," Saurush said. "What else could it be? An enforcer has no purpose for visiting a human college campus, unless it is being attacked by terrorists."

"He has more in common with you than he has with me, Saurush. He watches them, just like you. He did not make the enforcer's choice."

"Really? I thought it was mandatory for enforcer's to forfeit all memories from their mortal lives."

"If it were mandatory," Aadesh said, "it wouldn't be called the enforcer's 'choice', now, would it?" Saurush nodded. "Yes, good point." He looked around, assessing the mortals scrambling to get to their seating places. "It seems our peers have left for the day. I see only mortals apart from us."

"They left because they finished their day's work. And I'm stuck here with you, chatty Cathy."

Saurush kept looking around, until his eyes were fixated outside the window again. His jawline stiffened and eyes became narrower. "He's gone."

"He's not gone," Aadesh said, poring over his ledger's previous year's records. "He noticed we were looking, so he must've changed vantage. He's still somewhere looking at us, but we wouldn't be able to see him." Saurush sighed and continued scanning the surroundings. "No use looking. You'll never find him once he goes into stalking mode. Besides, it seems your mortal benchmate is here."

Saurush tilted his head and looked at the classroom entrance. There he was, the mortal who shared bench space with the accountant. Dressed in a shirt that didn't go with the pants and shoes that didn't go with anything he owned, he still walked quite confidently. Dreamy? Saurush definitely thought so. The boy wrote a lot during class hours, just not what the instructor was teaching.

"Distraction is my food for thought"

A pretty good line to begin with. A suppressed smile turned up on Samved's face as he etched the words absentmindedly on his register. Business Studies wasn't exactly the favourite subject as far as he was concerned, so that's how the class usually went. Given away to the higher calling. Creative hunger had always been his weakness anyway. Whether it be the inexplicable itch to make the most innovative science project or the insatiable craving to put ideas to paper, Samved had all symptoms of the disease fondly known as unbridled imagination. If creativity is a drug, then he was a dope by all means.

Not that you could tell by the way he looked. He wasn't the funny distracted-looking guy who'd be seen staring blankly ahead but seriously lost into some other dimension. The moment the skinny girl sitting next to him started to ask him a doubt about the ongoing topic he had nervously pointed out towards the board and given her a brief explanation. The teacher noticed it and explained the topic again. That was him, a calculative genius on the outside but a wandering poet on the inside.

"Maybe another reason to be writing"

He didn't hear the bell going off; neither had he cared about the crowd that left his side. Soon, he was sitting alone in the classroom. That had been the pattern of his life since as far as he could remember. His cell phone vibrated inside his pocket. He picked it up to be greeted by a message.

Radhika: hehe :)

Hi lips twitched, then twisted into the most pleasant curve.

"So you've finally gone mad." He typed and sent the message. His phone beeped again. Conversation was underway.

Radhika: I was mad since birth. Right now I am just expressing myself... hehehehe...

Sam: lol.

Radhika: I am wandering in the Delhi Haat.

Sam: Idle girl. You don't have anything to do?

Radhika: Nope. Haha.

Sam: Try and study someday. That is why you score so poorly in your tests. Its doctors like you who forget their phone inside a patient's kidney.

Radhika: Shut up, alien. You also never study.

Sam: That's what happens when an IITian gets in MBA.

Radhika: Go out and watch a movie, my depressed friend. Are there no mad people in your class?

Sam: No can do.

Radhika: My group is full of crackheads. By the way, I want to ask you a question. Why did you start writing?

Samved hesitated for a moment.

Sam: It helps me maintain my patience. Plus, I love it.

Radhika: Amazing. Hence proved... LHS=RHS... You are an alien. Generally, people become writers because they want an identity but they are not very good at anything else...

Sam: Good one!

Radhika: Okay! I am doing a research. I decided to write for a magazine during these holidays. HOLIDAYS!

Sam: Don't rub it in, medical college. This is literally the only time ever when you get a holiday and I don't get one.

Radhika: Fair point. Okay, next question. Why did you choose English as a medium? Why not Hindi?

Sam: I use both. I still write in Hindi. But I find English more comfortable.

Radhika: Okay... But if I say that, like any other Indian, you think in Hindi then translate it before writing; which means you lose some basic essence of your thoughts, is it right?

Sam: No. I can express myself better in English. Besides only 14% Indians communicate in Hindi, so let's not misrepresent fact. 'Native language' would be a better fit in that question.

Radhika: Okay, nerd! 'Native language'. Next question. Why are you so shy of people?

Sam: I am not.

Radhika: Oops! Let me correct myself. Why are you shy of girls?

Samved was stumped. He typed something, but kept on deleting it.

Radhika: Are you there?

Sam: Yes.

Radhika: You are a fool, Samved. You are so talented, so good at heart, and a topper, but you still can't tell Paridhi that you love her.

Sam: Are you crazy? I haven't ever talked to her.

Radhika: Then what the hell are you waiting for? Go and talk to her.

Sam: It isn't that simple.

Radhika: Why, what is the difference between me and her? You never hesitate talking to me. :)

Sam: You won't understand.

Radhika: You are a jerk. Both you and Ritesh are dumb-heads.

Sam: Good. Thanks for the compliment. Although I would prefer not being in the same sentence as Ritesh.

Radhika: Stupid jerk.

Samved left the class cursing her. He wasn't afraid of girls, but it is different with the one you love. Heart is the biggest enemy of the tongue.

On his way through the walkway next to the bicycle parking, he felt a chill pass through his abdomen and back his spine. He looked behind, coming face to face to face with the setting sun. Dusk was approaching. He had spent too much time on that poem. But now that it was already late, he decided to watch the sunset.

Rohit kept running even though his pursuer had long vanished. He thought he was going to bump into a strange clumsy person who behaved as if he was blind or something. A boy comes running towards you, you at least flinch and attempt to get out of the way. Not that man. He just kept walking straight into him. Rohit had no idea how he didn't crash into the man's abdomen. Anyway, he had other things to worry about.

It was strange, his heartbeat hadn't elevated even a little. He didn't feel out of breath either. His feet barely hit the pavement as he ran. The actual surprise, however, was the experience he had on the road outside the college. Not a single person in the entire crowded vicinity had so much as looked into his general direction even after his repeated cries for help. So he just kept running. His mind wouldn't allow him to slow down even for a second. His day had been scary enough already.

A sharp pain in the shoulder stopped him in his tracks. He felt an irresistible force pull him off the ground and haul him in the air. His eyes dropped slightly as he saw a large, shiny blade emerged out of his chest as he hung. His hands reached to grab the blade out of instinct, but he knew it was over for him. What terrified him, though, was that there was no blood even though his heart had definitely been stabbed. Instead, some fluorescent fumes or vapour leaked out from him, going off in evanescence. He summoned the courage to make an attempt to wrestle out of the scythe that had impaled him, but he couldn't. A hand grabbed his other shoulder and pulled at him, driving the blade even further. Rohit screamed louder than he knew he could. The tears in his eyes flew incessantly and his limbs twitched. No use.

Another hard tug followed. This time the hilt of the blade hit his back and the assaulter planted the pole of the spear into the ground, leaving Rohit hanging like a hunter's trophy. His screams didn't stop. His feet didn't stop shaking. The violence had been too much for him to handle. Not to mention, he could see four yards of a huge, curved blade right ahead; four yards of a blade thrust out of his chest. The hand holding him up eventually backed away, as his cries turned into mere sobs and his violent thrashing about faded out until only a slight twitching could be observed. The actual end was yet to come, but he knew that his story was over.

His murderer finally walked up in front of him. This would be the first time that Rohit was seeing the person, the first time he had merely seen the scythe and made a run for his life. The person was dressed in a big black robe. The hooded robe covered the entire body of the person, not leaving even the hands or the feet visible to an onlooker. The robe, added with the scythe, gave an unmistakable likeness to characters of ghost stories. Quite convenient for someone who spends their time killing people and hanging their bodies on a scythe. A closer look revealed that it was a woman.

"Are you…the Grim Reaper?" Rohit asked.

"You can call me that, but where I come from, I am called an enforcer."

"An…enforcer?"

The enforcer removed her hood and looked up at him. Her long, satin hair jumped out at her sides, making waves in the wind. Her eyes were green, but everything else about her face was rather common. Beautiful, but common.

"It can't be," Rohit groaned. "You can't be a Grim Reaper. Grim Reaper is all skeleton. But you are a human."

"I am not human, and neither are you."

Rohit gasped. He couldn't digest what he just heard.

"What do you mean?"

"It's such a pity," the woman sighed. "You are just a kid. How old were you?"

"I am twelve years old."

"Oh poor child. You died so young."

"I haven't died yet. You are the one trying to kill me."

The woman shook her head and held his hand.

"Haven't you realised it yet? How can you not see it? I have impaled you but there is no blood. No pain. You are screaming so desperately but no one can hear you. That man behind you is looking at you and smiling, because he doesn't see you or me." Rohit turned around, his eyes meeting the eyes of the clumsy man he had nearly bumped into. No. Not nearly. He had bumped into the man. And passed right through him. "He just sees the sunset behind us. You ran so much but didn't feel any fatigue, and you don't have a heartbeat or a pulse. What would it take to make you believe that you are already dead?"

Rohit's eyes expanded and his fists clenched.

"No...this is wrong...this...this...can't be..."

"You still don't believe me? Fine, tell me boy. What is the date today? What day it is?"

"It is 29 October, 2014. Today is Wednesday."

The woman shuddered. A smile waltzed across her face as she laughed on the very two facts that Rohit could swear upon. A newspaper came flying from across the playground. The woman caught it and held it wide open for Rohit to read.

"I may be a mysterious creature, but even I can't bring a newspaper from the future into the present."

Rohit choked upon his very voice. His eyes darted across the scrawny little page from a national daily as reality unfurled upon him.

4 November, 2014. Tuesday.

"No…this is…im…impossible."

"I think you need an explanation. Luckily, I have one for you. You think that today is October the 29th, don't you? That's because you died on October the 29th in a car accident. You received blunt force trauma as your skull was bashed into the windshield of your car and then into the ground. Death was immediate. But your soul didn't realise that you had died because the accident had been too sudden. Since your soul never came to terms with your death, your spirit couldn't leave into the afterlife. That is why I am here. To free you."

"I…don't want to…I don't want to die."

The woman held his hands again, pressing them this time.

"But you've already died. Now you just have to move on. And don't worry. Everything is going to be fine. Trust me. Please."

"I trust you," Rohit said.

And at that very moment, the spirit of the boy named Rohit dissolved out of existence. The blade vanished and the handle retracted until the scythe became a baton. The enforcer tucked it inside her left sleeve. Another robed figure appeared next to the her. White robe, blue cuff stripes.

"You wasted a lot of time today," he said.

"I'm sorry, Captain," she shook her head. "They were little kids. I thought their final thoughts shouldn't be of fear and hopelessness."

"Your orders, Lieutenant," the Captain roared, "were not to comfort dead kids. Do you realise what you've cost us? You were supposed to make short work of these 'kids', a simple task, and join up with Squad 11 in their hunt.

But since you'd rather play with souls instead of following orders, I had to assist 11 myself. Even so, by the time I reached them one soul had already escaped. You have made me look like a fool here."

The Lieutenant drew her hood back over her head. "I'm extremely sorry, Captain. I have made a grave error. I will accept any punishment you deem fit."

The Captain looked at her in silence. "The punishment should fit the crime. Your incompetence led to a soul's escape." He produced a file from the folds of his robe. "Shruti Singhal. 24 at the time of death. Your orders are to find her at any cost. I hope you are up to the task, Lieutenant. Remember, the pride of Squad 13 depends on you making this right."

"Yes sir. I understand. I will find her and finish the job."

Two accountants observed as the enforcers zipped away from the concrete walkway next to the bicycle stand while the mortal lumbered away in the opposite direction. The sun had set.

"Just another day at work," Saurush sighed.

The Assignment

"You are the boss. You have to *behave* like a boss. *Act* like a boss." Samved was busy giving himself the necessary instructions before he faced her again. Meanwhile, he failed to notice Radhika entering his room. This was not the first time she had crept up on him and quietly tapped his shoulder to give him a jumpscare. This had been the norm rather than the exception. And like the norm, it always got him.

Samved jumped and fell down on his bed in surprise. Radhika was laughing like crazy. But the real embarrassment was seeing his mother, who stood there laughing alongside.

"What the hell mom?" He barked.

"Et tu Brute, mom!" Radhika laughed. "Then fall Sam," his mum joined her, and both of them exchanged a high-five. "Literally," Radhika had her thumbs up. "Good one, aunty."

He could watch those two go at it forever. Those were the only two people in the world who could troll him and get away with it. Well, truth be told, a lot of people trolled him and got away with it in the sense that there was no retribution. Sam was a nervous wreck after all. These two, however, he loved them to pieces. They had the license.

"Hey," he got up indignant, "you should be on my side mum."

"Shut up, mama's boy," Radhika cut him up. "You still need your mother to face a girl? That's such a shame!"

Samved looked at her with a squint, and turned to his mother. "Okay, A. That is sexist. Girls can be as mean as guys. And B. There is nothing wrong with consulting your mother in matters of national security, which means saving my dignity in this case."

"What did we do?" she said. "As a matter of fact, it is us who are the victim here."

"What? Really?" A stumped Sam said. Radhika was beaming ear to ear now, her pearly teeth threatening to illuminate the entire room. "Don't act as if you know nothing" she said, and Samved's mom nodded. "You are practicing in front of the mirror for facing your subordinate. This is ridiculous."

"I wasn't practi…"

"'*Behave like the boss. Act like the boss. You are the boss.*' Who said all this stuff?" Checkmate.

"Listen, Samved," his mother's voice devolved into a raspy baritone. "Get this clear and straight. I will not find any girl for your marriage. So make your move on this girl and bring her to me."

"Be quick about it," Radhika added.

Sam stood transfixed at his place, cold sweat breaking out of his brows. They looked at each other and started laughing again.

"Grow up, my dear," mother said, brushing his hair with her hands, "You are a smart boy. Try and be confident as well."

Sam wasn't sure about what he'd say, but he had resolved that he would talk to Paridhi. He had given a long hard thought to his mother's words. He had been infatuated with this girl since his days in the B-school. Paridhi, the girl who had emerald green eyes, the girl who laughed the loudest, the girl who had curly hair streaks which changed colour every month. He had observed her, respectfully, from a safe distance. She had great ambitions. She was a bit clumsy but made up for it with sheer hard-work, and she had an annoying boyfriend who had some kind of pretentious name. Sam had every contour of this girl's face committed to memory, but could somehow not remember the name of the guy associated with her. His name started with the letter 'a'. Perhaps. Didn't matter, though. The guy didn't stay in the picture for long. They had an epic breakup, or so was the story. Sam graduated with his MBA, and his junior of interest stayed in his poems but not his general vicinity anymore.

Until she joined Goldman. As his subordinate. She had casually walked into his cabin one day, as if led by a trance of his unseen poems, and he couldn't get his heart to calm down until the HR came in to introduce the new girl. Over the next few days Sam realised that Paridhi didn't remember who he was. Or, to be more precise, she had never known who he was. Not that it mattered, it was all water under the bridge. He had been given a new chance to get to know this girl. He just needed his wits to stay with him when he looked at her.

Sam and Paridhi had spent three months as colleagues. It was socially acceptable to speak freely with her.

"Good morning sir," Paridhi greeted him with her regulation smile when she entered his cabin.

"Hi. I think you went through the statement for our next assignment?" Formal stuff, you can't screw that up.

"It's nothing special, sir. I looked into the details at length, and it seems to be pretty much identical to our last client's requirements. I think I can handle this stuff on my own. You'll have to throw some signatures here and there, but I'll do the rest."

"Okay, but don't overburden yourself," he said with concern.

"Oh, it's nothing, sir," Paridhi giggled a little. "I'll manage." She was fiddling with her hair. He had seen this before. He knew what it meant.

"You seem to be worried," he said unconvincingly, as he was no better himself. "I may be your lead but you can treat me as a friend. You might not have noticed but we did our post grads in the same year."

Paridhi smiled through the auburn tresses, an unusual hair colour by Paridhi's standards. "Thank you very much, sir," she said. "That puts me at a lot ease. By the way, I had no idea that you knew me before."

"Well, you were my immediate junior in MBA. So, yeah, I knew you."

"Wow, I wish I had met you then. You're really nice. Actually, my problem was a bit personal, and I thought it wouldn't be appropriate if I talked to you about it."

"I say it is quite okay," he replied coolly.

"Sir," she said. "I've heard you graduated as an engineer in Electronics from IIT Delhi."

"As a matter of fact, I did."

"My younger brother is also doing electronics in NSIT."

"Oh, that is good."

"That is my problem, sir," Paridhi frowned. "He got an assignment two months back, but he wasted the first two weeks. Now he says he can't finish the project himself, and he is very panicky. Besides his ideas are a bit over the top, would be an understatement. I am very much concerned about him."

"I can understand, and I think you would like me to help."

"I don't want to trouble you," Paridhi held his hand. Samved could swear he heard what she said next, he could argue that he nodded which proves he was listening. But his brain's processor had suddenly hanged, and Paridhi's words had never reached beyond his stunned ears. "Sir," she shook him, and he suddenly realized that he was supposed to listen.

"Oh," he said. "Don't worry. I have some bandwidth available for the next three months. I can help your brother handle his...erm...assignment. But I need to know what he was thinking about."

"I'll give him your number, and you may talk to him when you're free."

"Tell him to feel free to call any time after five. I don't sleep before two at night anyway."

"Thank you very much, sir," Paridhi held his hand again. This time Samved held his nerves and didn't go blank. "You've done a great favour to me."

"It's not a favour," he said softly, trying to breathe and control his pulse, "And you don't need to thank me. Now, let us get back to work. We got lots to do."

Nothing worth mentioning happened that day in the office, but Samved was in deep stress. He had promised Paridhi that he'd help her brother. This was his chance to be of value to this girl he liked, and he didn't want to screw it up. Twelve hours went by but his stress didn't.

"Did you talk to her?" Radhika said as soon as he picked up her call. Samved looked at the clock. It was midnight.

"No," he answered smugly.

"What?" Samved could make out from the voice that Radhika had jumped out of bed. "You are such a loser, Samved. You can't even..."

"Shut up crackpot," he intervened. "I didn't complete my sentence. I was saying, 'No. *She* talked to me.'"

"God damn it. Are you kidding?" Radhika's disbelief was heard for miles.

"She even held my hand."

"Shit! Don't tell me."

"Twice!"

Never had the word 'twice' invoked a better reaction.

"Whoa! My rookie has become a champ overnight. Congrats dude!"

Samved was smiling like crazy. Blushing, no need to mention. He would say more, but a vibration almost threw the phone off his hand.

"Oops," he said. "Hey, Radhika. I'll have to talk to you later. I am receiving another call."

"Oho, it must be Paridhi. Never mind. I won't play spoiler in your romantic midnight chat. See ya!"

The other call was from an unknown number.

"Hello!"

"Hello. Am I talking to Mr. Samved Singh?"

"Ah, yes."

"Good evening sir," the voice on the other side was shaky, but quite deep. "My name is Karan Mehra. I am Paridhi's brother. She is your subordinate"

"Yes, I know. I was expecting your call. And by the way, it's 'Good Morning' already."

"Err…Sorry sir. I shouldn't have called right now."

"No it's okay. Don't worry. You were troubled by your assignment, right?"

"Yes sir. I put myself into a soup."

"What were you planning to make?"

There was a long pause on the other side.

"Don't hesitate," he tried to reassure the boy.

"Err…My project…was to make…a device that can see ghosts."

Sam listened to the boy with absolute silence as he explained the idea of a device that could theoretically reach out to the supernatural and help mankind connect with the dearly departed.

"And you believe that this is feasible?"

"I think yes, sir," the boy said. "You may think I am crazy, but I have done some research. Metaphysics states that says dogs can see ghosts, because they see certain wavelengths that we don't. It is assumed that ghosts are a form of energy, just like we talk about a person's aura."

"So," Samved deduced. "Your logic is that if we make a device that can detect all possible electromagnetic and sound waves, we may see and hear ghosts?"

"Yes sir. I know it sounds crazy…"

"No. It sounds interesting. But don't you think that your idea can be presented to be more appealing to more traditional faculties?"

"I didn't get you."

"See, I say this not as an engineer but as a manager," Samved explained. "Never reveal the motive behind your work unless and until it is unavoidable. You want to make a device that detects obscure signals, to quote your project in layman terms. Now it doesn't matter what you intend to see with that device. It could be used for N number of applications. The fact that you want to use it to detect ghosts, I'd suggest, keep it to yourself. Present your idea as something that is mainstream, and keep your not-so-mainstream motivations to yourself. What do you think?"

"Oh! I think that is a good idea. I can do that. That will work."

"Okay! And if, at any point of time, you feel the need of my inputs or help, feel free."

"Thank you very much, sir."

"Don't mention it."

"Good night sir."

"Good night. And good luck."

Samved put down the phone but couldn't sleep that night. He was lost in thoughts about mother who was sleeping in the adjacent room. How many nights had he woken up to her nightmare-induced screams? How many times he had seen her crying all alone? Death was an unforgiving foe to every human alive. No doubt that a young boy wanted to look beyond death, maybe even find a cure to this terminal affliction. Sam went to the kitchen, hoping that it was just thirst keeping him sleepless. It wasn't. An idea, once it lands in the head, cannot be kicked out. It is an unwanted tenant that has to pay no rent. A tenant you have to keep. He had received one such tenant that night. Maybe it was childish, but it is easy to be childish when you see other juveniles. Sam could not let this go. He had made himself a promise, years ago, a self assignment, that he would defeat death. Fate had brought him back face to face with it.

The New Mission

Ghosts are nothing but a form of energy, as metaphysics states. It has been observed that a person's weight gets reduced after death. This is attributed to the mass-energy equivalence. When a person's soul or spirit leaves his body, it results in a loss of mass. But in most cases, the amount of energy released is not sufficient to cause observable change in mass. In a very few cases, which can be safely termed as rare exceptions, the loss of mass is nearly up to one and a half kg, which means that an enormous amount of energy(of the order of several million electron-volts) was released. This gave rise to the soul strength theory, which assumes that spirits vary in strength and energy. This is the reason that a very few spirits are able to make their presence felt to humans. It is also believed that the mode of a person's death and his mental state at that point of time decide the nature of his spirit.

No scientific research has satisfactorily explained the reason behind why dogs start barking even when there is nobody around. Owls also start screeching at night. Metaphysics says that this is because dogs and owls have their audio-visual senses operating at different frequencies than that of humans. They can detect energies that we can't and, apparently, ghosts may exist in a form visible in those energy profiles. In other words, dogs and owls can see and listen to ghosts…

"Damn!" Samved was scared by the knock at the door. He tiptoed towards it and slowly opened the door. The girl on the other side gazed back and blinked rapidly.

"Have you gone crazy Samved?" Radhika said "Why do you look so scared?"

"For a moment there, I thought you were a ghost," He whispered.

"What? You called me a ghost?" Shouting was imminent. "Aunty! See, Samved is saying that I look like a ghost."

"Hey, come down," he grabbed her arm. "Mom is not here. She is off to Jalandhar to attend my cousin's marriage. Took off in the morning."

"You didn't go?"

"No, I have an important project coming up. It was impossible to get a leave. Besides, she has gone for a full month."

"I wonder which part of the marriage takes one month."

"Divorce, I guess."

"Mean comment," she pinched him. "But why didn't you tell me before? I'd have brought you some dinner."

His jawline tightened. That smile had to wait. "It's time I started cooking for myself."

"Oho, big boy," Radhika gave him a pat on the back. "Seems like Paridhi has waved her magic wand at you. My mama's boy has suddenly grown up and wants to do the one chore he would never be caught dead doing. One of these days your mum will have tears in her eyes. Then she'll say 'Kids grow up so fast. My Samved used to be so little. And it feels like just yesterday'."

"Careful, Radhika. Nobody will protect you if I knock your teeth off today." He punched her lightly. "Hawww," she squealed and launched her hands at him. He knew where to tickle her to put her down, however. Soon, Radhika was asking for a timeout.

"Okay," Sam said. "Jokes apart! How was your day?"

"Oh, I almost forgot to tell you," she chuckled. "Dad returned from Vancouver today."

Sam's eyes widened. Radhika's dad. When was the last time he had seen him? Graduation day in school? The month after that, on her birthday? No. He definitely was there when Radhika got jaundice in her second year of graduation. "What? I thought he was coming next week."

"That is what he told us. But he was planning a surprise for us. You should have been there. We were all sitting on the couch, mum, me and Anuj. Dad entered and all of us stood up with our mouths open. We were ogling at him like fools."

"Hehe… So, he must've bought you something?"

"Of course," she jerked her head in attitude. "I'm his dearest. He brought my favourite Ray-Ban glasses. See!" She produced a pair of funky looking sunglasses. Samved noticed that another piece was lying inside her bag. "He brought two?"

"Yep, he sent one for the grown up child as well." She grinned, putting the glasses on Samved.

"Damn," she said. "You look so dashing in these. I feel like giving you a kiss."

"Go and brush your teeth before that," he giggled.

"Shut up yaar! I am giving you a complement and you are still making fun of me." she produced a sulky frown, as if on cue. Yes, she had a repertoire of expressions for every situation.

"I am just kidding," Samved said, hugging her. "By the way. You are my dearest too. You are the only girl who thinks that I am smart."

"Now don't start singing your tragedy ballad again, alien," Radhika pushed him. "And your dearest is Paridhi anyway. She has overthrown me a long time ago."

"It's not like that," he explained. "Nobody can take your place."

"Yeah, I know that. By the way, now I want you to wear these frequently."

"Your wish is my command, ma'am," he bowed.

"Good… Now go and bring some Maggie. At least I can cook that for you."

Radhika left after having a nice dinner, a couple of hours later, while Samved got back to work. A sudden idea had excited him up. What if he could make a tiny receptor which could detect all energy waves, and incorporate it into the glasses that Radhika had just given him? There couldn't be a better way to go about doing it. If it could detect ghosts, it would be the breakthrough he had been looking for. If it couldn't, it would be an amazing piece of equipment still.

Bright ideas suddenly accelerate the rate at which a task is approached. Samved was overjoyed at the thought of making a device which could see ghosts. There was only one major hurdle he had to overcome. How would he make such a detector?

The next day, Samved finished his work early and came back to his home. He threw his bag on the sofa and directly made way to the store room. He impatiently rummaged through his long forgotten belongings and, after a lot of searching, produced an old and dusty box. With a deep sigh, he blew the dust off its surface and opened it. It revealed a set of his old tools and instruments. Despite the time, the tools were in a perfect condition, a surprising thing considering that they belonged to the most careless owner. The shiny solder, which he had packed off about seven years ago, could be easily sold for new. And there were stacks of green silicon wafers and integrated chip-circuits he built during his college days. But he was mostly found working on other people's assignments, rather than his own. He realized he was doing the same thing once again.

Firstly, he'd make a prototype circuit detector. This test, if successful, would ensure that he was capable of making such a thing. Next step would be to reduce its size. Third step would be to put it in the glasses. All this looks easy on paper, but an engineer knows what it takes to build such a thing.

Over the following days, Samved's colleagues saw an unusual change in him. Suddenly, their talented but disinterested boss developed a love for his job. They had never seen him tackling the corporate problems with so much passion. He had been competent, but begrudgingly. Things were different now. Every day he finished his work in half a day, left the easy parts for Paridhi, and came back home to concentrate on his new invention. Success, however, never makes an anticipated entry.

Samved's efforts to make a detector failed again and again. He tried different circuits, different methods, searched and read every piece of electronics and metaphysics, but nothing proved to be useful. After two months of toiling, he was as clueless as he was before he began working on the project. There just wasn't enough research on metaphysics to allow for a pragmatic scientific enquiry.

Slowly, his life started drifting back towards the beaten path. He started handling his job himself, much to the relief of poor Paridhi. The time he used to give to his research declined geometrically, and he became the same dull guy he had been before.

"Why are a dog's sensory organs different from that of humans?"

Samved's eyes froze at an article published in his Reader's Digest one day. It was not an important one; it wasn't even there on the list given on the cover page. All it got was a small block tucked away in a corner of the index. He had never read Biology before, but now seemed to be the best time to begin.

Once again, Samved drowned himself in research. He realized the reasons for his failures and began inching closer to the goal.

"Switch off the door," he pointed his finger carelessly at the girl standing at the doorstep, carrying a plastic bag.

"Are you out of your mind?"

Samved turned and saw Radhika gaping at him.

"What?"

"You just asked me to 'switch off' the door?" She said "Have you lost it or something?"

"No, I was just working on something. My mind was somewhere else."

"Tell me something new."

"I am busy."

"I said tell me something new. This I've heard so many times."

He looked up with a frown. "What? What do you want?"

"I want you to take a break. Let's have a snack."

"Wait for a while. I am just finishing it."

"Shut up!" She took the solder from his hand. "I know how much time you take to 'just finish' your task." Samved was left with no options. It is better to surrender to caring girls before they lose their temper and become the sadistic devil. He stuffed a samosa in his mouth and began munching at it.

"What is the matter with you?" Radhika asked when she found him quiet.

"It's nothing. I am very close to something big."

"Well, good luck on that."

"Yeah, I need it."

"By the way, what is it? What are you working on?"

"It is nothing special. It's like a multipurpose detector."

"Okay, but don't neglect your health in the process. That reminds me, aunty is still not back. I guess the marriage should be over by now."

Samved sighed.

"The marriage is tomorrow. But she'll stay there for a fortnight."

"Why?"

"It's her home. She likes it there."

"What about you?"

"I am not a two year old. I can take care of myself."

Radhika looked at him and shook her head. "I can see that."

"Okay I can't, but you are here. She knows you'll handle me."

"I won't do that forever. That is why I came here."

Samved was confused.

"What do you mean?"

She stared at him for a while.

"I'll be leaving tomorrow. I am going to Dehradun."

"What? Why?"

"I am getting married, Samved," she grimaced. Sam tilted his head, processing.

"You had planned to wait for two years or so, if I am not wrong."

"I know that's not the question that you want to ask."

"You are aware that I know the answer," Sam smiled. "And you know I don't like it very much."

Radhika held his hand. "I know. And I didn't want to go so soon. I don't know how I'll live there. I will miss you so much, and aunty too."

"We'll miss you too, especially me. After all, who'll make that delicious Maggie for me when I forget myself in work?"

"That's all I am to you, then? You think I am your cook?"

"Now don't start all over again. You will be leaving in a few days. At least don't fight with me in these days. Especially given that I'm letting you marry *him*."

"If it turns out to be the wrong decision, I know you will be there by my side," she put her head on his shoulder. "Fighting with you is the one thing I'll miss the most. By the way, it has been a while since I asked you about Paridhi. How's she theswe days?"

"Fine, as far as I know."

"You know what I want to ask you. So don't act like you don't understand."

"Hey, I am just her boss. She treats me that way only. Nothing else has happened."

"So make something happen. Try and make progress. Do something to impress her. Get her attention. When will you approach her like a man?"

"I think I'll do that after you leave."

"And why will you wait for me to leave?"

Samved smiled smugly. "My marriage will give you an excuse to come back and meet me and mom here. Why waste that by making haste?"

"God, I can't believe I am speaking to Samved. Since when did you become so witty?"

"Remember the day when you stopped bathing? This happened right after that. And you smell just a little worse than a skunk."

"Mr. Samved, you are dead now," Radhika said, and attacked him.

After a light tug of war, both she and Sam settled down. She hugged him goodbye and left, Sam walking her to the end of the street. The adjacent plot was disputed land and, as a result, unoccupied. In the dark, it looked like a blanket of nothingness. Sam sometimes felt like the nothingness stared at him.

Keeping an eye on humans was beneath an enforcer, let alone an enforcer of squad 10. The Lieutenant, hence, wasn't quite pleased when she received a missive stating that she had to leave her operation and start observing an inconsequential being. Humans creeped her out. She had been recruited three years ago and she was told that new recruits often got orders to observe certain special humans. She never got such a job when she was a rookie. It made no sense to be relieved from a critical operation for something so trivial. But the Captain had told her that the mundane jobs were actually a blessing in disguise. Enforcers who did a lot of ghost-reaping had very little shelf-life. On the other hand, the more clerical jobs ensured survival and most top members in any squad were enforcers who had just sneaked up on unwary humans all their term.

Of course, she knew that was just propaganda to ensure she fell in line. The Captain gave her this job to punish her for the joint operation three years ago. Lieutenants didn't get mundane jobs. The Captain gave her this job to humiliate her. That human had been there, three years ago, she remembered.

"They should've at least told me the truth," she murmured.

"Well, I can help you with that."

The voice startled her. She unsheathed her Scythe in a flash, but the other presence grabbed the blunt end.

"Ease out Lieutenant," the presence turned out to be another enforcer. "There are hardly any creatures that can sneak up on an enforcer, especially here."

The other enforcer had blue stripes at the sleeves of his milky robe. The Captain, she couldn't believe her eyes. This could not be really happening.

"I'm surprised to see you here, Captain," she fumbled. "Surely, you don't think that whatever I'm doing here is more important than reaping operation?"

"It actually is," he replied calmly. "Not that it matters. I get an order, I follow it."

"Oh, are you here on some important mission?"

"Apparently, I am. I have a new order for you."

"New order; what is it?"

The Captain produced a small vial from the folds of his robes and handed it to her.

"Am I supposed to drink this?"

"No," he shook his head. "I am pretty sure it would taste quite horrible. You are expected to enchant something with this." He produced a file from the folds of his robe. "Rest of your directives are in the file. This is a top secret mission. You must ensure nobody, not even another enforcer, not even one from our own squad, gets to know about this. Is that clear?"

The Lieutenant looked at the blue seal on the file with the letters C-O-N-F-I-D-E-N-T-I-AL embossed in it. "I understand, sir."

"Then I will leave you to it." The Captain left as quietly as he had come. The Lieutenant opened the file while toying with the vial in her hands. Her eyes glided over the missive inside it. She read it once, then twice.

"I understand and accept my orders," she said, and the file crumbled away like sand in a breeze. She looked straight ahead, staying within the shadows even though she was invisible to the mortal world. A few paces away from her, her new mission waved at his friend.

Shruti

"What is the meaning of this, Captain?"

The Lieutenant's question was met with an outstretched hand. Without thinking, her trained hands transferred the file to the Captain's domineering palm. He casually turned his back on her, his white robe towering over her like a massive curtain even though his head was turned nose-down into the file.

"Looks like a transfer orders missive to me," he said. "It seems headquarters want you back on your old case."

The Lieutenant's hands were clenched tight, shaking. Her noses flared as she carefully enunciated her words. "I know that," she said. "What I don't understand is the reason behind this transfer. I was ordered to keep an eye on that human. Why has my mission changed now?"

"We don't question our orders, Lieutenant. Enforcers keep getting retasked and relocated all the time. There is nothing out of the ordinary here."

"Captain, with all due respect…"

The Captain turned to face her, his daunting eyes looking down on her. "Usually, the phrase 'all due respect' is followed by an utter absence of respect."

"You know what my previous mission was," the Lieutenant said. "Something is going on here, Captain. We are being kept in the dark. They are swapping me out so that I can't know what they've just made me do."

The Captain bent until his face was next to hers. "You're being swapped out because you are sloppy and rebellious, Lieutenant. You still haven't found out that soul that slipped away because of your poor decision making."

"I'm trying my best…"

"I don't want you to try," the Captain shrieked. "I want you to get the job done. Without asking questions that waste both of our times. Do you get it?"

The Lieutenant muttered, "yes sir." He handed her file back to her and dismissed her. She had no business with the human anymore, at least for the time being.

The following morning, Samved picked up his sunglasses and looked towards the sky. Dancing patterns of crimson, green, and blue lights greeted his field of vision.

"Cosmic rays. I can see…cosmic rays."

The rest of his day was spent in accidents. He alarmed half his neighbourhood by blowing his microwave just because he wanted to see the radiations more vividly. Later, he got involved in a brawl with the street dogs because he stepped on the tail of one trying to observe the invisible energies all around him. And street signs! He had no count of the poles he had run into.

"This is a great device," he said to himself. "It shows every damn thing. The only problem is that I forget to observe those things that everybody can see."

He had finally tasted success. He had made a device that could detect everything. Ironic that a pair of Ray Bans were the medium of this great invention.

Now all he had to do was find a ghost and make history. His search had to begin the same day.

A spirit's presence at any place depends upon the interest of the people in there. Spirits, being energy, feel the energy or vibes around them and are attracted by strong emotions like fear, anger, ego and frenzy. Dull vibes or disinterest usually drives them away.

Samved roamed around in the streets every morning, with his glasses on, looking for ghosts. His excitement was off the roof. Each day, he went to a new place, a new nook or corner of the city. He went to places he had never been to, places he'd never known existed. Each day he saw several people staring at him, or he'd run into trouble due to his carelessness. One day he found himself on the middle of the road crossing where the traffic came from three directions. God knows what saved him there. Three weeks of his hard-work produced just one result, though a very prominent one. Sun-burn!

His belief in the existence of ghosts was nearly shattered. He decided to give it a few more days, and then he'd submit the research for patenting. He went to his backyard looking for his 'butterflies'. He had always wanted to interview a ghost. He wouldn't leave that opportunity that easy.

He was just passing through the alleyway when he saw a girl coming from the opposite side. She looked twenty odd or something, extremely fair, and had a very attractive face. She had those big, black eyes that one could lose themselves in and supple lips which could kill if she smiled. She was in a red shirt and black jeans which definitely suited her. Samved almost forgot ghosts for a while. He kept walking towards her, expecting that her hands would brush with his when they would cross.

He felt a sudden chill when she passed across him. Samved cursed his luck as he had missed the opportunity to touch her hand. Dejected, he turned back to watch her go. To his horror, the girl went straight ahead and vanished into a wall.

"Now what was that?"

Samved was confused beyond measure. He had never seen people vanishing like that, and he was dead sure this was no illusion. It could just not be. There was no doubts about what had just transpired in front of his eyes.

Then he considered the last possibility that his mind had to offer. Perhaps, he had seen a ghost! The mere thought exhilarated him. He wanted to know more about spirits and afterlife. Who doesn't?

The next day, he went to the same place and waited all day. In the evening, the same girl appeared out of nowhere. He started approaching her. When he was at one step distance from her, he started walking backwards. There was no change on the girl's expressions.

"Hey!" He called out to her, softly. No reply.

"I am talking to you," he said again. No reply, again.

"Hey, listen you...RED SHIRT!" He almost barked. "I am talking to you. You think that I can't see you but I totally can."

The girl stopped abruptly. The stern expression on her face was replaced by squinty eyes and pursed lips.

"Can we talk for a minute?" He said. She kept looking at him silently.

"You can speak, right?"

There was no answer from her side. Samved became impatient.

"Can you understand what I am saying to you? If you can't speak, give me some gestures. I can understand sign language."

The girl gave him a one-gesture answer. She showed him the middle finger!

"Ahem…err…" he wasn't ready for this. "You want me to go leave you alone?"

"I think somebody said something about understanding sign-language." Finally, she had spoken. Her voice was very soft, but equally firm. Samved was really not in a position to talk. But he mustered the courage. It was a dead girl, after all. She had nothing to fear.

"But what is wrong? Why can't you talk to me for a while?"

"I might be dead," she said. "But I am still a girl. You can't just come up and expect that I will talk to you. And you were here the other day. I sense stalker behaviour. Not nice, pal."

"Hey, but you are already dead. I can't harm you in any way whatsoever."

"Exactly, you can't. But I can harm you in every way whatsoever. So you better take your mug out of my sight and stay the hell out of my way."

She turned to her left, nearly breaking into a sprint. Samved turned as well, but hit a pole and fell down. He sat up, rubbing his head. She was gone.

"What a ghost," he laughed. The whole day, he kept thinking about the short encounter with the most beautiful ghost one could run into. He definitely wanted to meet her again.

The next day, he was in the same street again. He waited all day, but the ghost had decided to give him a miss. Hell bent, he kept going every day. She didn't appear in front of him again. After a fortnight of incessant outings, Samved decided to leave her alone and get back to work.

"Hi," Paridhi greeted him when he entered his cabin the next month. "How's you?"

"I am fine," he smiled. "I reckon I have loads of work to catch up with. I've been slacking off lately"

"Yes, I guess so. You were scarce the entire past month. Some of us suspected you went and had an affair or something."

"I am sorry. I know I have given you unnecessary trouble."

"No, it's totally okay. That's my job. And now that you are here, we're going to do some great business."

"Let's get back to work."

After a long day of incessant paperwork and mindless presentations, Samved went home. He was surprised by the fact that somehow, his mad endeavours to find ghosts had diverted his mind away from Paridhi. He felt a bit guilty as well. If you are not thinking about the person you love some hundred thousand times a day then you are definitely in the wrong direction, or so he believed. Samved couldn't get that ghost girl out of his mind, much similar to what had happened when he had first seen Paridhi a few years ago. Fortunately, you can't fall in love with a ghost.

Consumed in those thoughts, Samved unlocked the door and entered his bedroom. He was taking off his shoes when he noticed the telltale chill in his room. The mirror on his dressing table was fogged. It was the month of July, and there was no chance of a sub-zero temperature in this part of the country. Besides, some of the mist on the mirror had been cleared. Smooth. Long strokes. Consistent with marks made by a small finger. Somebody had written something on it.

Put on your glasses.

Breathing heavily, he took out his anti-glare spectacles and put them on. He looked around, in vain.

The other glasses, idiot!

He was left gaping. He opened his drawer and pulled out his modified sunglasses. He put them on and there she was, sitting on his bed. It was the ghost girl from the alleyway.

"Why are you haunting me?" She immediately waved a finger at him.

What would be your reaction if you are arrested for your own murder? Samved's expression was no different. "What the...hey wait! *You* are the ghost. *You* are the one who is supposed to haunt. How on earth can I haunt you?"

"Hello Mr. Genius. You have all these Metaphysics books stacked up in your shelves and eating dirt. Do you ever mind actually opening them up and reading them? The book lying there on your study table clearly says that ghosts are attracted by interest. Let me give you some inside info. Outside the books. We are bound to thoughts. So, if you keep on thinking about me from day till night, I will be *forced* to roam around you day and night. Hence, I ask you a simple question. When the hell would you stop haunting me?"

"Excuse me," Samved said. "You can't order me to think according to your whims and fancy. You can't decide what I think. You are attractive. An attractive ghost. Anybody who sees you will keep on thinking about you."

An angry look waltzed upon the ghost's face. "If I could touch you, I'd slap the eyeballs out of your face. I am dead but that doesn't mean that you can flirt with me."

"See I am not flirting with you. I just want to know more about the dead and the afterlife."

"You are most welcome dude. Go ahead, jump from the terrace. You'll get to know everything about death."

"I am not joking here."

"Neither am I," the girl said. "You can't know these things and me telling them to you wouldn't make any difference."

"Why?"

"Ask something else."

"What is your name?" A simple question.

"Not your concern."

"Okay. How did you die?" A more demanding question. Sam knew she wasn't going to answer that.

"You are not getting an interview from me."

"See, you have to help me."

"What makes you think so?"

"I won't stop haunting you."

The girl's eyes enlarged to metric size. "Are you trying to threaten me? Listen here boy. I can kill you if I please, and no one can book me for that."

"Yeah, but you wouldn't."

"Don't go by my looks," she said. "I can do anything."

"Go ahead then." There was a long, uncomfortable silence. Sam was very much afraid. She was a ghost after all. She could actually go ahead and kill him.

"Okay, I'll help you." The girl snarled with a defeated finality in her voice.

"Yes!!"

"Just this one time, though. And I am not answering any personal questions. Don't ask me anything about death and ghosts. I'll do anything else."

Samved sank into his chair. "Are you sure?"

"Yes, except killing somebody or something bad, I will do pretty much anything."

"I will definitely not ask you to kill people or stuff like that." There was another long pause. "I have a simpler question for you. What do you think about me?"

"What kind of a question is that?"

"Just tell me. What do you think about me?"

She nodded her head for a while. "I think," she said, "that you are a very resourceful person who takes advantage of somebody's ill situations."

"Ouch, that hurt," he beamed and chuckled. "Anyway, that is not what I want to know. I was asking that what kind of impression I leave on you?"

"Okay!" The ghost shook her head. "Now I understand. This is about a girl. Has to be about a girl."

"Yes."

"You like her, but can't tell it to her?"

"Exactly!"

"And you want me to help you get close to her."

"That's right. Please don't refuse. I love her since past four years."

The girl turned quiet. "Okay," she finally said. "What's her name?"

"Paridhi," Samved smiled.

"Nice name. And you are Samved? The guy who has no human friends so he nags dead girls to help his romantic life, or the absence of it."

Sam laughed. "Yeah, that pretty much sums it up."

"Alright, but let me tell you one thing. This is the only thing that I will do for you. After that we go our separate ways, and you never ever think about me."

"Yes, I accept your terms."

"You won't disturb me again."

"Never," Samved shook his head.

"Promise me!"

"Nope I won't, never in my entire life. I just want you to make me good enough for her."

Another solemn moment followed. "You love her so much?"

"You've got no idea."

The girl smiled.

"May I know your name?" Samved asked.

"No," she answered, still smiling.

"So what do I call you, Banshee or Miss Dead Inside? Pick one."

"Shruti," she muttered. "We'll begin tomorrow onwards. Now chop chop. Go and catch some sleep."

"Good night," Samved exalted, taking off his glasses. "Shruti."

Project Paridhi

The streets of Hazrat Nagar were more or less deserted. Most of the people were off to work, and the mood of the festive season was concealed in the lull. Luckily, Samved had nothing to do with live humans at the time. He put on his glasses and looked around.

"There you are," he exclaimed as he identified the ghost he was hoping to see. "What's up?"

"Shut up," she said. "Don't try to get friendly with me."

"What's wrong with…" he started speaking, but stopped when Shruti gave him the death stare. "You are a crazy girl," he sighed. "So, what are we doing today?"

"Okay, today I'll give you your first task," Shruti replied with a wry smile. "This street is all yours. Pick any random girl, and get her number within one week."

"What, are you kidding me?"

"Rule number one! You'll never question or refuse any tasks that I give you."

"So you ask me to jump in the well, and I have to jump?"

"More or less," Shruti grinned. "But wells are too clean to accommodate you. I'll rather have you jump in the gutter."

"No can do. The gutters of our country are already beyond dirty due to lack of cleaning. I don't want to make them worse."

This was the first time Samved saw her laugh. She had a strange vibrancy on her face, something that had been missing up until that moment. "You always act like that? You like making fun of yourself?"

"No but, anything for your smile."

Shruti giggled. "Second rule, don't ever flirt with me."

"Why don't you finish up with your rulebook all at once?"

"Rule number three," Samved tore some of the hair off his head when Shruti said this. "I decide when to reveal the rules."

"Whatever you say, ma'am," he said, defeated.

"Okay, go and do the task you've been given."

Sam had no idea what she was talking about. He just stared at her with a quizzical look on his face.

"It'll be better if you begin without my prodding. If I select a girl for you, you'll spend the rest of your week either crying about your dying wallet and running after her with a dozen of shopping bags, or get into jail or worse."

Sam shook his head as matter of factly as he could. "Damn, you're dangerous. I didn't know you could select these types of girls."

"You've no idea, pal. I might hook you up with a girl who'll get pregnant before you even come to know her name."

"Well that's nice, and undoubtedly impressive, but the girl I want to get doesn't belong to any of the above types."

Shruti advanced towards him in excitement. "A girl is a girl. She never belongs to categories. Stop thinking that all girls have to be treated differently, but don't do the mistake of handling every girl in the same manner."

Sam blinked. Repeatedly.

"Didn't understand what I just said?" Samved shook his head in response. "You won't understand," she smiled. "It's deep philosophy of female psychology."

"There she comes," Shruti hurriedly pointed towards the apartment opposite to Samved. A young girl, most likely in her early twenties, emerged. She was probably heading for college.

"Hey, don't try to drag me into this," Sam was indignant. "This girl is going to the college. She is way too young."

"Your birth certificate says that you are twenty-seven."

"You read my birth-certificate?"

"You have no idea, stalker. Go ahead now, no more excuses."

"I can't do this. You know it too."

"Come on," Shruti groaned. "Be a man. Don't back off like that."

Samved didn't budge.

"Alright," Shruti spoke in a guttural undertone. "You leave me know choice. Take off your glasses."

"What?"

"Your glasses, darling, take them off. And observe the young lady. I'm sure that you can do."

Sam obeyed without further questions. The young college girl was walking towards him at a confused pace. She was on the phone, probably talking to her friend. Then, she stopped abruptly. Her body jittered a little, she dropped her haunches, and broke into a sprint . Her feet were unsteady, so she stumbled. It was a bizarre turn of events. She hit a pole straightaway and fell down.

"Oh, damn," Samved cried and rushed to help her. "Are you okay?"

"Give me a hand, idiot," the girl grunted.

Samved threw his hand towards her without much thought. "What happened there?"

"I am not quite used to controlling a body," the girl answered.

"What," Samved was utterly perplexed, "are you talking about?"

"It is me. That's why I asked you to take off your glasses."

"Shruti, is that you?"

"Yeah, it's me," she said. "What did you expect? I guess that is what I need to do to make you comfortable with girls."

"You can control bodies?"

The girl looked up at him with her large eyes. "Seriously," she shrieked.

"Yeah, I didn't know."

"I am a ghost, you dumbass," she continued. "That is…what I should say… natural stuff."

"Well, I had no idea about that."

"These are the perks of being dead."

"That's good, but if you can control bodies, why don't you possess one forever?"

"That is not possible smarty. Living human bodies are compatible only with their own soul. A ghost can only possess a body for a small period of time. If the foreign spirit doesn't leave a given body after that amount of time, it will result in destruction of both the foreign soul and the body's original soul."

"Hey but souls are energy. How can you…"

"You're not getting past the point, my friend," the girl interrupted him. "Spirits are not just any energy. They are much more than energy. Technically, spirits are organized clusters of different types of energy."

Sam could not help but gape. "Wow, how do you know so much about spirits?"

"I *am* one. Plus, I was a student of metaphysics. In fact, I developed quite an interesting theory about spirits and ghosts, and I found it to be true. Unfortunately, I had to die to verify my theory."

"So sad," Samved sighed.

"Oh come on," the girl spoke hoarsely. "Stop playing the pity game. We've got work to do."

"What work?"

"Oh, I am sorry Samved. I just forgot to tell you."

The girl stepped back, and presented her hand to surprised Samved. "Hi, I am Nisha Chandra. I am Karan's girlfriend."

Samved shook her hand, but the quizzical expression on his face was still unchanged. "Who is Karan?"

She slapped her head with her palm. "Karan Mehra, idiot, he is Paridhi's brother."

Samved's mouth opened and refused to shut back. "I can't believe it. You... how could you...how did you figure that out? You picked up Paridhi's brother's girlfriend? That's just…"

"Unbelievable, isn't it?" Nisha laughed. "Well, let's just put it this way. I studied some case-history before I stepped in."

"You are the height of anything," he gasped.

"I know that, Sam," Nisha smiled. "Now I have to figure some way out to help you befriend Nisha."

"I don't think I follow you."

"Nisha is the key to open Paridhi's heart for you. She can say what you never dared say. She'll tell Paridhi everything you want her to know."

"How do you think shall we do that?"

"You just do what I tell you to do right now. I can't possess Nisha forever. We'll talk about this later."

"Okay," Sam nodded. "I'll do as you command of me. Now what's the plan, Shruti?"

Nisha looked at him with wild eyes. "I'll go up and jump from the first floor."

Sam freaked out before Nisha could narrate the rest of her plan. "What? Are you out of your senses?"

"Shut up," Nisha screamed. Seeing this, the watchman ran up to Sam waving his stick and threatening to beat him up like a stray dog.

"Hey you," he shouted. "Don't try to irritate our *Madam*. Don't worry *Madam*, I'll handle this fool."

"SHUT UP, BAHADUR," Nisha was on the verge of blowing out her diaphragm. "He is my friend. I can handle him. You don't dare put your leaky nose in between."

The watchman stood stranded. He adjusted his pot belly around his belt.

"Now what on earth are you waiting for?" Nisha cried.

"Nothing *Madam*," the watchman replied.

"Then please leave, Bahadur," she whimpered.

"*Madam*, I think you are not well. Please come with me immediately. I'll call the doctor."

"Shut up Bahadur," Nisha was seriously pissed. "You are the one who needs a doctor, you idiot. I told you to LEAVE."

"Okay, it's fine," the watchman lowered his head. "I will leave."

"Oh God, thank you very much. You've just saved my life."

"But…"

"What?"

"My name is Ramdin," the watchman spoke in a louder tone. "Not Bahadur."

Sam burst out into laughter. Ramdin turned and went away, leaving Nisha and Sam staring at each other. After a few seconds, she took his hand and they walked up to the first floor of the building.

Sam screamed in a whisper. "What, are you crazy? You really are jumping off?"

"Listen. The fall is not going to kill Nisha. She'll get unconscious, and the watchman is already out of our way. So you go up, pick her and take her to the hospital. When she wakes up, all she'll know is that she had an accident and you saved her life. Nice way to get introduced to someone, isn't it?"

"Yeah, very well, but you don't need to create all this fuss. I can simply go and meet her. I mean it will be a fine intro anyway."

"Oh yes," Nisha sighed. "I forgot that you are the dumbass Samved."

"Now what did *I* do?" Sam whined.

"Come on yaar," Nisha exclaimed. "Don't be so stupid. You'll just go and say - 'Hi, I am Samved. I am your boyfriend's sister's boss' - and you expect a girl to hit it off with you? Listen, girls don't care about dudes who approach them like that. If you want to talk to a girl, do it without any references or connections. That is why I made this plan. Now don't waste my time. I told you I can't possess her forever."

"Okay," Sam took a deep breath and nodded. He had understood most of what Nisha said, or at least he *believed* he had.

"I'll jump now," Nisha said, and climbed up the railing.

Sam was looking at her clueless. Nisha kept standing up, trying to gather the courage to jump. "What are you waiting for?" Sam poked her from behind. "You're already dead, remember?"

"You are most welcome to come up and try yourself" Nisha turned and replied. Sam shrugged.

A moment later, Nisha stuttered as if somebody had electrified her. Her body began shaking. "Oh my god," she cried with a clear change of tone. "What on earth is going on? What am I doing up here?"

Sam was alarmed. Shruti had warned him already about the fact that she could possess a body only for a while. The plan had definitely failed. Nisha was awake and was about to turn behind. Sam's nerves suddenly took over. A strange instinct propelled him, and he lunged forward with a dash. His hands delivered a big push to Nisha's already unbalanced body. She fell down with a thud on the ground below and slipped into oblivion.

"Hey you," a loud scream ringed into Samved's ears, but it was the eyes that bulged to react to the fact that somebody had seen him push a girl off the building. His teeth jammed against each other due to the shocked reflex of his jaws. "You pushed her off. I saw you. Somebody call the police. Somebody…" Sam knocked him down. It just took one sturdy right hook. The fallen guy was a tall, thin-built person, but he seemed to be rough and tough. Well, not anymore. Sam ran down, picked up Nisha's unconscious body, deposited her in the backseat of his car, and took off to the hospital.

He kept on cursing the entire way. "What the fuck?"

After admitting Nisha in the hospital, he called Paridhi.

"Hello Sir, what happened? You got late and…"

"Hey listen to me," Sam said. "I just had an accident here."

"Oh my God, is everything fine? Are you okay?"

"I am completely fine Paridhi. The accident didn't happen to me. Some girl fell off a building. I brought her to the Forbes' hospital."

"Forbes'," she reciprocated. "Okay, wait there. I am coming."

"Alright, I'll see you. Bye."

The doctor came out of the room.

"Hey doctor! How is the girl?" Sam asked.

"She's fine," he replied. "She fell unconscious due to shock. She is wide awake now. You can even take her home, although I'd not recommend that because she broke her leg."

"Can I see her?"

"Yeah sure, please go."

Sam quietly opened the door and entered the room. Nisha was lying on the bed and constantly tapping her mobile phone with her thumbs. She was texting. He sighed.

"Hi," he said when he realized that there was no other way Nisha would notice him.

"Oh," Nisha looked confused. Her voice was weak. "Do I know you?"

"No," he shook his head. "But I sure know you."

"Really, is that so?"

"Yeah," he said smugly. "You are a struggling stuntwoman."

"No," she was confused even more. "I am not a stuntwoman."

"Then why did you jump off that building? Don't tell me that you were trying to commit suicide because your boyfriend left you."

The girl wasn't amused. "Hey, my boyfriend loves me a lot. He can't leave me. As a matter of fact, he is on his way here. He'll reach any time."

"That's exactly what I was missing here," he muttered under his breath.

"Sorry?"

"Oh, it's nothing." Why was the phone ever built? Screw you, Alexander Bell!

"By the way, I didn't jump from the building. Someone pushed me. Bloody son of a…"

"Don't curse, please!"

"Why shouldn't I?" Nisha frowned. "I broke a leg here. I was trying to lose weight, and I was dieting, exercising, doing all that stuff to stay in shape. Now, I am on a hospital bed with a broken leg. By the time I lose this plaster, I will be a warehouse of fat."

"Well, that's sad," Sam inserted his puny three word sentence, which was lost somewhere in the sea of a girl's grievances.

"And that fool even touched my ass."

Sam's expression was full of penance. "I'm sorry," he said. "I have a question, though. What were you doing on that railing when that…that person…whoever it is…pushed you?"

Nisha shrugged. "I've got no idea. I was going to college. Then I felt some kind of a jerk…and when I woke up…I was on that railing. I…I've no idea what happened to me. And I have no idea why I am telling you everything."

"It's okay. Maybe it's because of the shock. I once fell off my bike on my way to coaching class. I got a hard hit to my head. Then, I went and attended the class. I spent six hours there, chatted with all my friends, and solved every single question that was discussed. But after I woke up next morning, I remembered nothing of the previous day."

"Yeah, but who are you anyway?"

"I am the person who brought you here," Sam answered confidently. For the first time since he had met her, he was telling the truth.

Nisha looked at him with a strange, enquiring expression.

"And," he continued with a shaky voice. "I didn't touch your ass."

The door jolted open and a guy entered inside in quite a hurry. The same guy who Sam had knocked down earlier. Nisha's boyfriend. Paridhi's brother. "Nisha, are you okay...what the...you?" He spoke in a flurry of words, hardly understandable, and then pounced and caught Sam's collar.

"I'll break your bones you bastard."

"Hey, you back off right now," a shrill voice entered the room and filled it with so much force; it felt as if the hospital had experienced a thunder-strike. Karan backed off, whimpering like a puppy who had been hit badly by its oppressive owner. Sam turned his blue face towards the red face which had just saved him from a good beating. Paridhi had arrived.

"Paridhi," the guy said. "This guy pushed Nisha, and then knocked me down."

"Oh really," she screamed even harder. "How can you even believe that *this* guy can knock *you* down?"

"What?" Sam looked at Paridhi with shock.

"I mean," she clarified, "he can certainly knock you into tomorrow, but he's a gentleman. He can never be so brutish. In fact, he is the one who brought her here."

"You know this guy?" The boy left Sam's collar and walked up to his sister.

"Yes," she nodded assertively. "He is the person who helped you finish your project and saved your ass. He's my boss."

Karan was stranded. He placed his palm on his forehead and kept it there for an eternity.

"Nisha, are you okay dear?" Paridhi broke the silence and sat on the bed, stroking Nisha's long hair.

"I am fine, but that leg will keep me down for a while."

"Oh, don't worry about that honey! We'll take care of you."

"I am so sorry sir," Karan said. "I was actually…mistaken by your shirt. The person who pushed Nisha also wore a blue checked shirt just like yours, and very few people in this part of the city can afford Peter England shirts."

"Oh it's okay," Sam faked a cool response, after a moment of pause. "I would've done the same thing if I were you. There are indeed very few people who wear Peter England. But what I am wearing right now is a designer shirt, and if the person you saw wore a shirt *just* like mine, then Peter England are about to lose some business."

"Oh you shouldn't pay attention to him," Paridhi said. "He has a bad memory, especially when adrenaline is pumping. Not to mention, he was knocked down." A forced smile came on Karan's face.

"I guess I'll be leaving now," Sam fetched his car keys. "I'll come with you," Paridhi said, getting off Nisha's bed.

"No, please, you stay with…Nisha…right?"

Nisha nodded.

"But sir…"

"Take it as an order, Paridhi," Sam said. "If you'll call me sir, then I'll give you orders. Fair enough, isn't it?"

"Okay, Sam, wait," Paridhi stopped him once more "The files are in the third locker from the left in the cupboard, upper compartment. And the…"

"I'll call you," Sam interrupted her again. "I have a bad memory too." He took his leave and exited the hospital.

As he opened the car's door, Sam put on his glasses. "How can you even believe that *this* guy can knock *you* down?" Shruti appeared in the backseat, imitating Paridhi. She burst out into laughter.

"Hey, shut up," Sam grunted. "I did knock him down. Anyways, you don't talk to me. You did everything to screw me today."

Shruti's laughter was ringing into his ears. She wasn't going to stop in near future. "I am sorry dear," she said, suppressing her giggles. "But I must say this. You've got guts, and you've got wits. Today, you used both of them very nicely."

"Thanks for the compliment," Sam turned a sore face towards her.

"You impressed me today, Sam. You made those split-second decisions, and you never hesitated for even one moment. You are a very confident liar, I must say."

"Yeah, but I hate lying," Sam said. "I also hate doing these crazy things."

Shruti nodded, still smiling, ready to double up laughing anytime.

"So? What's the plan now?"

"You'll have to get closer to Nisha."

"Why, she's not my point of interest," Samved questioned.

"She is *near* your point of interest," Shruti explained. "To get to Paridhi, you've got to earn Nisha's trust. She is her best friend."

"That's not true," Sam said. "I am her best friend."

"You are her boss and don't know squat about her. Besides, a boy and a girl can never be best friends."

"No, that's not true. That is just what people say…"

"Shut up," Shruti's tone elevated, leaving Sam quiet and angry. "I know better than you. Just do what I say."

"Say," Sam said hoarsely and stopped the car. "I am listening."

"Sam, I didn't mean to…"

"Just say what you're supposed to say. No bullshit."

"I just don't want you to make mistakes and lose your love," Shruti spoke in melancholy. "It is a burden you'll never want to bear. Trust me; I know how it feels to be a failure in love."

"Why don't you tell me?" Sam asked quietly.

"I won't. I can't. I'll tell you some other day."

"I don't have many friends."

"I have no friends at all," Shruti frowned.

"You must have had friends when you were alive."

"I had friends. I also had a lover. When I died, neither of them wanted to see my face. I'd perhaps hurt them too much. I'll just call it their kindness that they cried at my funeral."

"I don't know much about you," Sam sighed, "but I think you must've been a very nice person, because you still are. And for the record, never say you've no friends. You have me."

She looked up with a smile. "There is just one thing that I know about myself," she said. "I screwed up my life."

"Well, all of us are screw-ups in one way or the other."

"You are a very sweet guy," she spoke very softly. "That is the sole reason why I agreed to help you in the first place. I don't want you to end up breaking your heart, but you are very naive. You need somebody to take care of you."

"So, finally you're telling me what you think about me."

"You've got to trust me."

"I do trust you. That is the sole reason why I ever asked you to help me in the first place. The point is, do you trust me? Would you tell me your darkest secret? What holds you back, what makes you behave differently from your real self?"

"I…I need time to do that."

"It's difficult to follow you blindly, after all that happened today. Still, I'll try, seeing that I've got no choice. I am too dumb to win the heart of any girl." Sam had misted eyes.

"No, you're not one piece dumb. Don't ever think like that. It's just that you get nervous when you're with people. You forget your real self in the pleasantries. You just need to be a bit spontaneous, like you were when Nisha was standing there on the edge of the railing. You need to be a bit casual, like you were when you talked to Nisha and her boyfriend. And, most importantly, you need to be a bit smart and reckless, like you were when you knocked Karan down."

"I don't know. I've never had the confidence."

"Oh you have it. Anyway, even if you lack in confidence, what am I here for?"

Sam looked up with a strange smile. He didn't speak, because somehow, he knew Shruti wanted to speak.

"You know," Shruti continued, "death sucks. I feel all alone, all messed up, and there's no one who'll ever find out what am I going through. It becomes all the more difficult because I am a girl. You see, we're always insecure, unsure of ourselves. We're capable of giving infinite love and care, but we need incessant inputs ourselves. We need to be cuddled, to be told again and again that somebody's there for us, somebody who would love us despite all our flaws. I won't create a general image, but that is what I - in particular - feel. There are times when I become so much depressed that I need someone's support to just continue with whatever is going on. I want somebody to hold my hands, or caress my hair, or simply give me a tight hug and tell me that everything's fine. 'It's alright. I am here.' It can't happen. It's just me and a void that I created for myself. Sometimes I just want to cry, but I've no tears to shed. So I just end up smiling when I am sad."

"It's alright," Sam whispered. "I am here. I can't hold your hand though, but I'd love to. I'm sure they must've been very soft."

The sullen look on her face suddenly changed into a beautiful smile. "I told you not to flirt with me."

"That's the one rule I can't follow," Sam grinned. "Let's be friends, shall we?"

He opened his palm towards her.

"I think yes."

Nisha slurped the tasteless soup and clicked her tongue, staring blankly outside the window. There wasn't anything to see though; heavy morning fog reigned supreme in the atmosphere. The cold came as a complementary to the fog, complementary, because the fog was more dangerous than the cold itself. It reduced visibility to barely a couple meters, making travelling quite dangerous. The fog was the reason why Nisha had to grow up without a mother, or so she had been told. She didn't have many fond memories of her father too, but she did remember the way he had described his wife.

There are many forms and types of love, but the love Nisha had for her mother was probably the most amazing love story she had ever known. Loving a person you never met or knew, just fashioning a sweet face and clinging on to that imaginary portrait, which becomes an artificial memory with time. The fog reminded her of her childhood, and the struggles she had to go through to find her way out of the fog of confusion and restrictions life had flooded into her existence.

The nurse switched on the television but Nisha asked her to turn it back off. She just wanted to look outside. Although there wasn't anything one could see, but the mere idea of 'looking outside the window' gave her a feeling of freedom and power. She was in a small room with a plaster cast over her leg; a sense of freedom was something she needed more than medicine.

"Hey, big girl," Paridhi broke her chain of thoughts as she rushed into the room. "I have been told that you are doing well."

"Don't give me that shit," she replied without looking. "I have to stay here for a month or so, and that's not exactly 'doing well'."

Paridhi shrugged and sat next to Nisha. She gave a good look to the food-tray on the table and nudged Nisha lovingly.

"Being upset won't help your leg. And eating this tasteless soup, and that too cold, will not help either. Here, have an apple. Sam sent you an entire assortment."

Nisha looked at the apple and smiled. "It seems like your boyfriend is pretty caring. That's nice."

"He isn't my boyfriend," Paridhi frowned. "He is my boss. And we are just friends."

"Great, so you do like him?"

Paridhi lowered her head and tried to produce a counter-argument, but Nisha had gotten all the evidence she needed. She gently lifted the tresses off Paridhi's face and winked. "Sweet, a workplace romance is under way."

"No, it isn't like that. I mean, he is my boss. He is a very nice man, but he is just friendly and all. I don't think he has any other ideas."

"Oh, he has many other ideas Paridhi. That man wants to sleep with you. Whether it is for one night or for the rest of his life needs to be found out."

Paridhi forced an apple into Nisha's mouth to shut her up, but not before she was pink with shyness. "You are drawing too much out of this. It isn't like that. I mean, we have only known each other for a few months."

"So it is just a matter of time before your boss gets under your dress? Not bad. He really has you in his claws. I bet he thinks of you every night when he, you know, wink wink."

"Nisha, now you are taking this too far. You know how much I hate it when you dirty talk, and I especially don't want to hear any crap about Sam. Eat this apple and try to talk sensible."

Nisha took a mean bite and turned her gaze at the window again.

"I know how much you hate when I dirty talk, that's why I dirty talk with you. I like the way you react to it, all matured and protective and awkward. You know, you are a sister to me, and a sister is the closest thing to a mother that I can have."

Paridhi stared at her for a while, brimming with tears.

"I think I just made a touching childish dialogue. Now you will hug me or do you need a written invitation?"

Paridhi couldn't stop her laughter. Nisha had a way of changing the mood of the party at will, and nobody was immune to her charming immaturity. Paridhi drew her into a warm hug.

"No surprise that your boss likes you," Nisha murmured. "You have such a perfect figure."

"Stop it now," Paridhi pat Nisha's back. "That's not how you are supposed to talk to the closest thing to a mother that you have."

"Actually I can," Nisha chuckled. "There is no generation gap between us. Now, your boss seems to be quite interested in taking care of me. Let me see what kind of a person he is."

"See, I like him," Paridhi sighed. "But I am afraid. I don't know what to do next. He is very sweet and charming and magnetic. He's just a child who wants everybody to be happy. But after Abhimanyu, I don't know….it's become too hard to let myself fall in love again."

"Fuck Abhimanyu," Nisha shouted a whisper. "He was a lying, cheating son-of-a-bitch. And he was a past that didn't deserve you. That's why he is nothing but a repressed memory. And your boss doesn't seem a single bit bright, so I don't think he can fool you. Nobody can fool you, you just see right through people."

"Abhimanyu did."

"To hell with Abhimanyu. Why do you bring him into this conversation? If you want time, take it. If you want to be surer, so be it. Your boss doesn't even know what you feel for him. Don't behave all childish and confused."

"But I am childish and confused," Paridhi pleaded. Nisha understood her at once, because she could see a very familiar look in Paridhi's eyes. The look she had hidden behind plastic smiles for so long. "He is unreadable. He just jumps from one task to another like nothing else matters, but he is so considerate and nice and perfect. No amount of time I spend with him will tell me anything new. I will need to make a move, or wait for him to make one. It's so confusing."

"Okay, stop," Nisha held Paridhi by her arms. "My God, they should reserve a bed for you too. You're shivering. Your boss is bad for your health."

"I've only known him for a short while, but he has gotten under my skin," Paridhi's voice cracked away. "All my life I have just taken care of Karan. That's all that mattered. I never knew that I'd get so used to the way my boss treats me. He just overloads me with his extra work, and then clears out the road for me. He lets me earn my promotion and prove myself, but he treats me like a princess too. I have become dependent on his way of letting me choose my way of life, and then ordering me around to work hard for it. I shouldn't."

"It's not wrong to depend on somebody if they are worth it. No matter how independent I am, I do depend on you, and I can accept it because I trust you so much. About your boss, ask him to visit me. And don't worry. Everything will be fine."

Paridhi couldn't speak further. She had always shied away from everything in life and focussed only on Karan's happiness and her own career. It was time that she had a life-partner. Samved Singh was a candidate, but he had only been with her for a while and she was thinking too far ahead. She simply hugged Nisha and cried for a minute, then left for the day.

An hour later, Sam was at the hospital to visit.

"Come in," Nisha waved at him after he had apparently been standing at the door for an entire minute. "You could've knocked or said something."

"You were busy with an important text, I assumed," he sat nearby. "The doctor said you are recovering faster than expected."

"I am sure he said the exact opposite," she frowned. "I overheard the conversation."

"Well it was worth a try. They say that a patient's state of mind affects their recovery. It is called...placebo effect...I think."

"I see you brought me something. Fruits. Apples?"

"Yes. Apples it is." Sam opened the paper-bag he had and produced a sturdy red apple. "Care for a bite?"

"Shouldn't you wash them first?"

"Oh, my bad. I am sorry." He fumbled with words and hurried towards the wash-basin a few paces away from the bed. Nisha looked on, but suddenly convulsed and shook violently.

"Hey," Sam left the bag of apples at a table near the basin and rushed towards Nisha. "Are you okay?"

Nisha opened her eyes smirking. "Never been better." The change of tone was immediately noted and recognized. "Shruti?" Sam shrilled.

"You shouldn't use my name so liberally," Nisha answered. "Not many people are familiar with ghosts, so they'll think of you as a lunatic."

"What is with you? Why did you possess her?"

"One of the many effects of a ghost possessing a human is that if the possessed human is sick or injured in any way, they get healed faster. The way I see it, it's win-win for all of us."

"Point made," Sam relaxed. "So, anything you want me to do?"

"Be quiet for a while," Nisha's voice was subdued by the munching.

"What the hell?" Sam almost jumped off. Nisha was eating an apple. The only apples Sam knew of were at the far end of the room.

"How did you get that apple?"

"I didn't. The apple got to me."

"What do you mean?" Sam was beyond shrugging. He was just too utterly confused.

"I am a ghost my dear," Shruti said. "I have a special power that allows me to create spatial anomalies which makes it possible for me to…let's say… teleport, stuff and stuff."

"Spatial anomaly, what are you talking about?"

Nisha stared at him haplessly. "Seriously dude, you are hopeless. For all the research you did on me, you know nothing about metaphysics. There is a theory that all elements of space and time coexist at one single point and are connected by anomalies. If you could figure them out, you could travel and send things beyond the physical barriers of space and time. I know about space, still working on time."

"You didn't tell me that ghosts could do that."

"Not all ghosts can," Nisha interjected. "Possessing people is a power that all ghosts share. Apart from that, every ghost has a special power, a Singularity, which only a rare few others possess. My Singularity is spatial anomalies."

"Oh God, you're awesome!"

"Why did you come here?"

Sam got surprised at the question. "What?"

"You heard me" Nisha repeated. "Why did you come here?"

"I came here to see if everything was going fine. Paridhi was worried, so I dropped by to check."

"That's quite nice of you," Nisha ran her fingers through her hair bashfully.

"Tell me more about spatial anomalies."

"What? Well, I am not a Physics nerd."

Sam realized that Shruti had left. Nisha was back with him. The transition left him stumped, so he couldn't do much. He just muttered a red-faced apology and left the room.

The Invitation

"*E*nforcers," *Diya came in shouting. "They are planning to make a move today."*

"No worries," Raj said. "Shruti will give us a head-start on them."

Diya's power to access enforcer communications had been a precious boon. She could just tap in and give everyone a heads-up on whatever the enforcers were planning to do next. However, Shruti knew that her power to create spatial anomalies, which made her capable of travelling nearly as fast as she could think, was the main reason why their posse was able to evade the enforcers for well over two years..

"I don't think that will work this time," Diya replied. "It's Squad 13."

The chamber fell silent for a minute. Travelling right beneath the population of the city like nomads had been the story for all ghosts for as long as anybody remembered. The enforcers had never let them survive. As soon as the leader of a group grew old enough, the enforcers would reap all of them. This had been going on and on forever. Of course, some ghosts who knew the tact of survival would live despite all the odds, and these were the ones who'd go on to become too formidable to hunt. One such ghost was Anasuya. At 802 years, she was the oldest ghost known as per the enforcer archives. And she was the leader of Shruti's group.

"Squad 13," she sighed. "Their Captain and Lieutenants can follow

us through any spatial anomalies. And I am very sure they are coming today."

"What do we do now?"

"Since Shruti is the oldest one after me, she will lead you from here. I will buy you some time."

"No," Shruti protested. "We can't leave you here. They will…"

"Yes," Anasuya smiled. "Go ahead. They will what, kill me?"

"We can't just leave you here."

"If you don't, they will never stop following you. As long as you are with me, you are in grave danger. I can fight Squad 13 all alone, but you won't last a minute. So just go and stop worrying about me. Remember, you don't have a reason to stop running yet. I do."

Anasuya's plan could have succeeded. She really could take on an entire enforcer squad on her own. Except that there were two of them this time. Squad 11 had teamed up with Squad 13, unbeknownst to them. To add insult to injury, someone else was helping them. Raj, Diya, Lauren, Megha, each of them fell prey to the enforcers, one by excruciating one, until Shruti was all alone in the world again.

A splash of water across the face woke Paridhi up. She dropped the glass, which still had some water in it, on her feet and winced in pain. It took her a moment to recognize her own kitchen, but she was more concerned about the dream she just had.

"How did I reach here?" She grumbled, dazed.

She looked around alertly as a hunch told her that somebody was observing her.

"What the hell is happening with me?"

"I am sorry. Being a ghost, I need to possess people to have dreams." Shruti quenched her urge to answer Paridhi, although she knew that Paridhi wouldn't hear her.

"So, what's going on?" Sam asked.

"I am good, but you don't need waste your time seeing me everyday," Nisha said. "You've already done enough for me."

Sam shook his head. "Hey, you're like a sister to me. So don't even dare to stop me from taking care of you."

"You are very sweet," Nisha looked at him with a glowing face.

"Tell that to your future sister-in-law."

"I knew there was something brewing between you and Paridhi. Does she know about it?"

"No, didn't have the courage to tell her."

Nisha's lips twisted in a sinister smile, "Now this got all the more interesting."

"Would you mind telling me what's on your mind?" Sam questioned.

"I'll tell you, but not now. Just have a little patience. Once I get out of this stinking bed, Karan and I will give you some inside info. For the time being, I'll just say that you're in the right direction."

The smile on Sam's face was far wider than what it was when he had finally found a ghost, so it needs not be implied how happy he was. He had waited for some positive vibes from Paridhi's side for years, but had never actually hoped that it would happen. And now it was happening. Nisha couldn't be lying. In fact, she wouldn't tell him anything if she hadn't owed Sam her life. Girls might be known worldwide for gossiping, but most of them are pretty good at keeping secrets too, especially when it comes to genuine friends.

He left with a burden put off of his shoulders. Now that he knew, he could be more frank with Paridhi. The only problem was that neither of them had the time. Coffee at lunch-time, late-night chats, it was all well and good, but not effective. Sam needed to spend some quality time with her, but he had no occasion to do so. And although Shruti's idea had been an overall advantage to him, it brought a disadvantage too. Now that Sam had been introduced to Karan and Nisha properly, most of the time he spent with Paridhi was shared with these two as well. Somehow that was a nice thing as well; the real quality time with a man that a girl cherishes includes the time that they spend with the girl's family. He smacked himself. What had Shruti told him? He had been thinking so much. He needed to turn off his brain for a while. Too much thinking had never worked out for him, while recklessness had brought him success every time.

He was just about leaving the hospital when he received a text from Radhika.

Call me. It's very urgent.

He was surprised. Radhika never behaved like this unless something very problematic happened. He called. A strong noise made him put the phone away for a second the moment she picked up. The noise subsided slowly.

"Hello, Samved?" Radhika's voice was almost breaking off between her giggles.

"Hey," Sam said. "You texted me. Is everything okay?"

She started laughing.

"Yes, everything is fine. You haven't talked to me in ages, you idiot. I was having doubts whether you even remembered me or not."

"Oh." Sam sighed apologetically "I had gotten busy."

"As expected," her voice was exceptionally loud, which meant she was very happy. "You sound quite happy today."

"Look who's talking. Just hear yourself. You almost sound as if you are getting married this month or something, and you are telling me that I sound happy." There was an abrupt pause. "Hey, are you there?"

"What are you, a psychic or something?" Radhika was frenzied. "I was hoping to surprise you but you surprised me. Who told you about my wedding being this month? Was it Ritesh?"

She had expected Samved to react. As soon as she told him about her wedding though, the phone went entirely quiet. She looked at the screen; it read 'Call Dropped'. She dialed again, only to realize that Sam's phone had been switched off.

Meanwhile, Sam was busy assembling his phone aside the hospital. It had simply fallen off his hand, out of shock he believed. Radhika was getting married to Ritesh and it was happening within the month.

Although the news that Ritesh was getting married was a shock in its own right, because the only thing he did to live females was having mindless intercourse with them. Ritesh marrying Radhika was completely unexpected. Or not.

Samved was happy, beyond doubt. Everybody knew it. Paridhi knew it the moment she saw him in the office, Radhika knew it when she talked to him on the phone again later, and even strangers knew it from the broad smile he so religiously carried for days afterwards. His joy was infectious too, everybody got warm and positive around him. He was radiating excitement, to be exact. Yet, part of him conflicted with the very facts that had caused this utopia.

Shruti sensed this. Sam was on cloud nine, yes, but he looked around at trivial things with a strange surprise, as if something was out of place. He looked at the calendar and displayed utter shock, as if he had woken up after a hundred years. He checked everything around him. It was as if he was in a dream and was looking for a snag in the system, which would certify his doubt, and help him to wake up.

"What has happened to you?" She managed to pop the question one day. "You seem dazed all the time; as if somebody has dropped you behind enemy lines."

"I don't know," Sam barely said the words. His mind wasn't on the plane you could call earthly.

"I have gotten used to this behaviour of yours. Talking to me one moment, then drifting away into your own world. But this is different. It is as if you are…"

"Sceptical," Sam whispered "That's the word you are looking for."

"Yes, yes," Shruti nodded. "What is going on?"

"I find it hard to believe that Ritesh and Radhika are getting married."

Shruti burst out in laughter. If she had a body, it would have convulsed due to lack of breath. "Is that it?" Sam found it weird. Being a ghost, Shruti could laugh and speak simultaneously. There were no barriers of lung capacity. Sam had seen this many times, but whenever she did this, he got a little scared as well as irritated.

"How many times do I have to tell you?" He barked, jerking his head and covering his ears.

"Tell me wha… oh, shit," she replied, still laughing. "I am sorry. But I can't help it."

"You have no idea how frightening this sounds."

"Okay, cut it. So that's it? You find it hard to believe that Ritesh and Radhika are finally getting married?"

"Yes," Sam shook his head. "I don't know…"

"See, it happens. You are probably too excited about their wedding. That makes you a bit twitchy. That happens to everybody."

"No, it isn't that. It is not the way you think. I…um…I don't know…it's…"

"Relax man," Shruti's chilly form swept over him, a gesture that she was hugging him from behind. Another spooky manoeuvre of his ghost friend.

"Get off me, Jack Frost! It is already winter and I don't need a cooler."

She floated through his body and turned to face him. "Okay, listen. You are a bit nervous. Maybe you think that it is all happening way too fast. But it was you who told me that Ritesh and Radhika were made for each other and you couldn't see them with anybody but each other, wasn't it?"

"Yes, and I'll stick with my statement, no matter what!"

"So, what's the problem?"

"I don't know! I don't understand. I have a feeling that I saw something bad happen. Something happened and I was a part of it.. And now it seems like a very faint memory, like people remember their long dead grandparents. It seems as if I saw something detrimental happen to them, I was there, and then somebody froze those memories away with liquid nitrogen."

They stared at each other for a long minute.

"It is your common sense that somebody froze away with liquid nitrogen," Shruti said with a deep sigh. "Look at you. You talk like an idiot. If I were alive, I would…"

"Shut up," Sam got visibly angry. "Enough with this 'If I were alive' shit. You are more alive to me than most people I have seen and been around. You are the only friend I have apart from Radhika."

'This is exactly why I keep reminding myself of my death,' Shruti thought, 'or else I will fall in love with you.'

"Well, say something now." Sam's rebuke shook her off.

"Okay, I am sorry," she smiled. "Notwithstanding that, you try and keep these thoughts away. Everything's okay. Your best friends are getting married. Enjoy the moment; and a new order for you about the Paridhi thing. Take her with you. Attend the wedding. Marriages - trust me or not - are the most romantic conditions for a girl."

"And the most not-romantic conditions for a guy." Sam said with a smile.

"Now that's my boy," Shruti winked, and vanished. Another spooky manoeuvre of his ghost friend.

Sam switched on his laptop and made an entry under the title 'The Ways of The Ghost'.

"Day 37:

It's been over a month since I first met her. The ghost, named Shruti, has revealed a lot about ghosts and the dead, but I still have to know the capabilities of the dearly departed souls who are somehow left behind in our world. For a long time, man has been in awe of the most commonplace mystery of the world - death. It is not a surprise either since the very basic requirements for curiosity are fear and lack of knowledge, and death meets *both those criteria. We have always been overwhelmed by death because we don't know anything about it. We don't know what happens to a person once he or she dies. Of course, we have made many assumptions, innumerable guesses about the other side of life. But nobody has ever been able to explain death as anything but the absence of life. Although scientifically, that much should be enough. The opposite of white is black, and you can't define the colour black as anything but the absence of every single colour. Yet, life and death are a lot more complicated than a palette of colours. For the longest time, we have tried to get close to the understanding of death through some rare and unreliable incidents of people having out-of-body experiences. While we have, as scientists, made peace with the idea of spirits and their frequent trips in our mundane world, we have not yet resolved several religious and mythic assumptions that don't quite fit anywhere with what the modern findings can account for. But then, modern science can never account for anything at all, can it? So it all goes down to this, the only way to understand death is to go through it. I am positive, that if it can actually do any good, there has to be some science fanatic who'd happily take his life (or somebody else's, seeing the fact that it is much more convenient to kill somebody in your place) just for the benefit of science. Luckily, such an approach would only be fruitless (till date), so no modern scientist has tried getting blood on his hands. But what a lucrative chance would it be if a dead person comes along to tell you everything you want to know about the life beyond life. I read somewhere - "Scientists make the worst of poets." Perhaps it is our insatiable hunger for knowledge (that reigns supreme over every other instinct) which is mistaken for our coldness towards most other basic feelings. That's not the truth about us. In fact, that's the worst lie there could be. A crazy scientist isn't cold, he is just too concerned with the quest for knowledge that every other thing becomes a secondary. That been said, I can safely assume that I haven't yet become the crazy scientist. I still am a very illogical stupid human, thanks to the fact that there is something that I hold more important than knowledge. The people in my life. Every person has his priorities. Mine include my hunger for solving every mystery that comes my way, but I think living a happy life isn't necessarily living a curious one. My departed test subject, Shruti, taught me this. She was a fascinating scope of research to me in the beginning. But after all that I have been through with her by my side, I think she is one of the most important friends I have ever had. This was supposed to be a note, and I have already made it a diary entry. So I guess I won't hold back any longer and just go with it. Shruti has become another Radhika to me, another friend I can rely upon. She makes me happy, she makes me smile, and she helps me in getting the one person I truly love, Paridhi. Too intimate for a test subject, no? That's why I realised that knowing everything isn't necessary. That's why I have decided to not study Shruti anymore. Whatever she tells me from this moment forth, stays between me and her. Ghosts are a great topic for research, so I'll let other great minds handle this. As for me, I am quite happy just being a special person who has become a friend to a dead person. I don't need anything else to go with it. But then, a habit is a habit. So, I'll log down the most relevant findings about ghosts that Shruti provided me with:*

Possession: Every ghost has the power to possess a living human (but not a dead one). This power seems to have a time-limit, because the possessing ghost is compelled to leave after a certain lapse of time. But the act of possession doesn't apparently affect either spirit in a permanent manner.

Singularity: Apart from the power to possess people, every ghost has a unique power that they call Singularity. A Singularity is apparently a special power that very few ghosts have. Those who do, have only one Singularity, whilst there are nearly unlimited varieties of a Singularity. In other words, it is very rare for a ghost to have a Singularity, and it is even rarer that two ghosts have the same power as their Singularity.

Intangibility: Ghosts are not only invisible, but intangible as well. They can interact with matter at will, though, but they mostly wander the earth without so much as touching any material object at all. But when they pass through a human, an unmistakable chill can be felt, possibly due to the large amount of energy they are continuously drawing from their surroundings.

That is all that I have learned about ghosts by now, and that is all that I mean to log.

Apart from this, there is another problem that came my way. I have, more than once, tried to replicate my device that sees ghosts, but have not been able to succeed. This means that my modified Ray Ban sunglasses are the only known apparatus that can detect the presence of a ghost. There must be some environmental condition or some unknown factor that triggered the power of my device to see ghosts. That 'secret ingredient' is, as of now, missing and not identified. So it seems that my research is obsolete for now, because I can't make another device like this. I could try to take help from some scientists, but I want to do this on my own. So, my next log will be about the progress of my research exclusively about the device that detects ghosts."

End of file

The Endgame

"It's so much fun to play both sides," Nisha said, toying with her hair. "Love is the most entertaining game God made."

"You're such a terrible person, Nisha," Karan made a face. "Paridhi is so nervous because of Samved *bhaiya* and you are just enjoying the show on the side-lines?"

"Not the side-lines, stupid. I have a front-row seat. Besides, Sam and Paridhi are made for each other. There is no doubt that they'll soon confess their love to each other. But until then, we can watch them play dumb and enjoy the dilemma."

"You really are diabolical. You can make a terrible villain in any story."

"I know", Nisha smiled, lifting her blanket to slowly reveal her left leg. "And you'll be the naïve young man I seduce and manipulate."

"Like you haven't already done that."

Nisha giggled as Karan embraced her and peppered her with kisses. "Oh… stop it…this isn't the place for such things. Besides, I still have a lot of recovery to do."

"Yeah, don't worry. I am only going to do second-base stuff." Karan held her hands and kissed them.

"Okay, I'd love some second-base stuff. I have spent quite some time here and it's been really boring. And you couldn't come to visit me too, thanks to the exams. No surprise that I feel so slutty."

"Oh man, you are just unbelievable. How can you be so direct?"

"Yeah, yeah. Paridhi keeps scolding me for my incessant dirty talk…"

Karan scratched his head. "Wait a second! You dirty talk with Paridhi too? That's weird!"

"Well, she likes it, but doesn't admit it. These days it's mostly about Samved. He may look very decent and meek but I am sure that when it gets down to action, he'll turn out to be a surprise package. Besides, Paridhi has such a tempting body that it can bring the beast out of any man."

"You do realise that it is my sister you're speaking of? And you sound like you have some sort of fetish for her." Karan was smiling through his teeth.

Nisha held his collar. "Who would not have a fetish for her? She is so smoking hot, man! Sometimes I really wish that I was a man. I would give anything to be able to have her at least once."

"That's enough, you pervert," Karan shook her mockingly, and then tickled her until she was out of breath.

"Okay, time please," Nisha called out, still recovering from acute laughter. "If that's the second-base stuff you were planning on doing with me, I'm going to look for a new boyfriend as soon as I get off this bed."

"Yeah, I am sure you are. But enough messing around for now. Tell me seriously, what do you think of that guy, Samved? You've done a lot of talking with him recently."

Nisha adjusted her body as she sat straight up, flexing her muscles. "Relax, sweetheart," she whispered, caressing Karan's face. "Paridhi isn't just your sister. She's mine too. If Sam didn't seem like the most perfect man on the planet to me, I'd have driven him right out of Paridhi's life and not let him set foot within miles of her. The only reason I like him is because he is just too sweet, for reals. And Paridhi is head over heels for him. It won't be long before Sam gets that sexy hot bod all to himself."

"Yeah I will just disregard that last sentence. You have approved of him. So why aren't they together yet?"

"They are both nervous, terrified actually. That's the beauty of the whole thing. Both of them have feelings for each other but they have no idea how to express them. That's the game, and it will be fun to see how long they need to figure this out."

"Wow," Karan sighed. "You're smarter than I thought. I guess I am a lucky guy."

"Oh yes you are, tiger. Don't tell me you ever doubted that."

"I still am not able to understand one thing, though," Karan shrugged. "You know the entire situation very well, but you won't do anything to speed up what is going on. Why is that? I mean, you could easily save Samved and Paridhi from a great deal of anxiety if you simply conveyed their feelings to each other. So why won't you? It would be much more convenient, don't you think?"

"My dear beloved. That would be convenient for *us*, not for *them*. If you want a relationship to succeed, you must let it grow at its own pace and in its own way. Do you now understand why I persist at letting them sort it out on their own?"

Karan's eyes lit up. "You bet I do. You really are smarter than I thought."

"Squad 13 has mobilised," the officer reported. "They have entered the city and are awaiting further orders."

"Great job, enforcer" the Second Lieutenant smiled. "Now all that's left is to let things happen as will."

The Lieutenant placed the file on a desk that was lit with several square lights, each assigned to perform its function as a control key. The walls of the room were mostly masked behind life-like screens that observed each and every move the enforcers made, and more. The tower itself, the communication hub, was the most important beacon of the enforcer squads. It was the house where all enforcer intelligence was acquired and processed. The enforcers were divided into thirteen squads that shouldered the responsibility of reaping lost souls and maintaining the balance of nature, among other things. Squad 13 was the most elite squad. Their main job was to handle intelligence and perform top-priority ops that the other squads were incapable of handling. Squad 1 was the second in-charge which handled the judicial management of the enforcers and ensured that no enforcers would step out of line. Squads 2, 3, and 4 were punishment squads meant to carry out the sentences issued by Squad 1, and sometimes Squad 13. Squads 5 through 8 formed the Research and Development wing of the enforcer system. Their job was to develop enforcer technology and to handle any enforcer casualties. Squad 9 to Squad 11, were the secret operations squads. Their job was to carry out ops that involved high-risk ventures, generally for gathering intelligence for the higher squads or for playing decoys to lure out elusive spirits. The last of the enforcer squads was Squad 12, which was also the largest squad in terms of numbers. Their job was mostly to play foot soldiers and do the mundane patrolling and reporting, plus situation-handling. These thirteen enforcer squads were what stood between the human world, the spirit world, and total anarchy.

"The communications need some repair work done," the Second Lieutenant sighed. "And as we go about it, let's do some renovation too."

"Yes, Second Lieutenant. I'll push a letter. But you do realise that Squad 7 needs to approve the recommendation."

"Yes, yes...I know."

"There is one thing that I don't understand, though," the officer smirked. "Permission to enquire?"

"Granted."

"You asked me to acquire the Uncloaking Potion from the lab of Squad 6, and then ordered me to give it to a subordinate who would then deliver it to the Captain. Considering the fact that the Uncloaking Potion is an extremely rare item acquired from the Witch clan, and the fact that it is prohibited to acquire it without permission, let alone have it delivered in the human world, it is really surprising that you had me do what I did."

"Squad 13 is the top squad in the enforcer program. Even if I did follow protocol and seek for permission in advance, I wouldn't need to specify the reasons for which I needed the Uncloaking Potion. But given the circumstances, I couldn't waste any time pushing papers, so I just skipped the permission-acquiring step."

"Yes, I do understand that, Second Lieutenant. What I don't understand, however, is what use would the Captain have of it? And why would he not share it with any of us?"

The Second Lieutenant walked over to the chair and relapsed into it. "You have always been a great soldier, but there is a lot about strategy that you don't yet understand. Sometimes, we need to do something suspicious in order to get things done. Not to forget, our orders come directly from HQ. They decide what we do and how we do it."

"I think you are right, but I cannot do much about it. For as long as I remember, you have been the one giving the orders and I have been the one running headlong into battle. That's the way it has always been, hasn't it?"

"Yes, you do have a point. And you have been impeccable in what you do. Still, with the amount of time you have spent with me, one would assume that you would know how I think."

"I can wager that nobody can ever catch up with your thought process unless you let them. Anyway, the answer to my questions still elude me."

The Second Lieutenant stood before the officer, smiling in anticipation of the scheme that was about to unfold in front of him.

"Fine. I'll tell you. In order to answer you, I must ask you something. Tell me, how do you defeat someone who is too determined to give up? How do you crush an irresistible force?"

The Lieutenant scratched his head for a moment. "I don't know. In fact, as far as I can think, there is no possible way to defeat someone with an indomitable will, unless we just kill them. But we aren't allowed to kill humans."

"That's right. There is no way to defeat someone who will never give up. And there is an enemy who will never give up unless they get what they want. So, we helped them."

"You helped it because you couldn't defeat it? Somehow, I don't see the logic behind the plan."

"The logic behind the plan is, that if you want to defeat someone who won't accept defeat, the only way is to make them believe that they have won. While they bask in the pretense of victory, they are exposed and that's how you beat them."

The officer nodded in realisation, and sighed in pleasure. "I think I understand now," he said. "You gave the human a false pretence of victory so that he may neglect the more threatening truths within his reach."

"That's wrong, officer. It is not about the human or that runaway spirit. The Witch clan's magic may be breathtaking, but once they share their recipes, our Research and Development squads find out the trick behind it in a matter of hours, if not minutes. It is a small price to pay for a big mission. The human, he is just a piece in play. He is not the endgame."

"You refer to the human as him. Why is it that you address humans as they matter, unlike other enforcers, who just refer to them as if they are objects?"

"That is because I am one of the very few enforcers who know who these humans really are and where they come from. If you knew that, you'd never speak of humans as inconsequential beings. Alas, it isn't something that you are supposed to know."

"I see, Second Lieutenant. I suppose it would be a waste of time for me to investigate further? Those of us who made the enforcer's choice don't really understand what makes the basis of your motivations. I have realised, however, that most top ranking enforcers are ones who didn't make the choice."

The Second Lieutenant nodded. "Keen observation. There's a good reason behind that. Some things are beyond principles, officer. That's why I am more afraid of humans than I am of rogue enforcers. Enforcers who made the choice are mostly simple, devoid of emotions and curiosity and resolve. They just follow obligations without doing anything extra. Humans, on the other hand, are much more complicated. That is why they must be surveilled regularly. After all, they have been kept oblivious to so many truths that eventually, one will find something. That is the endgame. Information is the real asset that we want to protect."

"Apples again," Nisha scowled at the basket she just received. "I am sick of apples now. Why can't you bring something like, pomegranates?"

Sam rubbed his stubble for a moment. "I'll remember next time."

"Yeah, and you said this the last time too."

"I know that, dear. I am getting forgetful these days. And my job is not helping."

"Don't give me that," Nisha frowned lightly. "Paridhi works a lot more than you do, and yet she takes better care of me."

"Don't compare me with *her*. She is too perfect to be a human being."

"Yeah, she is a smoking hot piece of pie."

"Ahem…I think you should not talk about her like that."

"Are you kidding me? You should be the one talking about her like that. I am just taking the pressure off of your shoulders."

Sam mocked her with a plastic smile, ironical, for the most part. He carefully placed the basket at the table and sat beside her. "Just a week now," he said. "Then you'll be out of here."

"Yeah, I am excited about that. I'll miss this place too, though. I met some really nice people while I was here. There was that kid with thalassemia, who would just never stop making fun of people. I really hated him at first, but then somebody told me that he had only a few months left to live. I sometimes wonder how these doctors live with all this going on around them. I saw that kid three or four times and I just got so attached to him that I can't bear the thought of never seeing him again, never seeing that smile, never being laughed at by him. How can the doctors live with this? They must have been around him for like hours and days at a stretch."

"That's why people don't like coming to a hospital. Apart from a miracle or two, all you see here is pain, suffering, and death. The doctors do whatever they can but there are people who just can't be saved. I too, could never understand how these doctors make peace with the fact that there is another human who is going to die under their observation and there is no way that they can change it. Maybe they just do it over and over again so often that their mind becomes used to such tragedies. One of my best friends is a doctor too, a surgeon. And she is getting married."

"Your friend is getting married? When?"

"Five days from now, I think. I forgot the date too."

"Some friend you are," Nisha shook her head. "So you will attend it, right?"

"Of course I will. I may have a terrible memory but I can't skip *this*. But the wedding is in Dehradun and I'll have to leave tomorrow."

"Great. Paridhi's also going, right?"

Sam squeezed a half-smile and swayed his head a little.

"You haven't asked her yet?" Nisha pinched his ear and shook him as hard as she could. "What kind of stupid are you? You have to take her with you. I don't know anything."

"But I don't think that she'll come with me. I mean, with your condition…"

"What condition man? I am not fucking pregnant or dying or something. Besides, my boyfriend is here to take care of me. You have to take her means you have to take her. I don't know anything else."

"Okay," Sam swallowed a lump in his throat. "I'll talk to her about it."

"You won't talk to her about it, you'll take her with you. If you, by any chance, attend the wedding without her, I'll never talk to you ever again."

"You really are an extreme person, you know that?"

"Yeah, I know. And you are a slow one. Do you want me to repeat what I just said?"

"No, I am good. I wonder why every girl in my life keeps bossing me around. Paridhi is the only exception, but maybe that's because she works as my subordinate."

Nisha held his hand and paused. "You don't know your own worth. That's why some people treat you like trash and get away with it. But Paridhi's feelings for you are very genuine, and they have nothing to do with the fact that she works under your command. I am a girl, and I have been her best friend for as long as I can remember. She used to be my tutor back in the days when she was in college. When she came here, I followed a month later, coincidentally. Karan had been with me for a year already at that time. I had my own issues back then, but Paridhi became an elder sister to me. That's why I let Karan into my life too. So, long story short, I can say that I know her better than anyone else does. And I know that if you ask her to go to a wedding with you, she'll not refuse. Now, are you going to ask her?"

"I think I will," Sam winked.

Questions

"Don't ask questions," Sam fluttered absent-mindedly "Just pack your bags, and come with me."

"But work?" Paridhi's question was deflected off Sam.

"What work?" He grinned. "Is there anything that you and I can't manage in half time?"

"Alright," she smiled softly. "No arguments."

"That's my girl."

Twelve hours later, they were already close to reaching their destination. The transcendental scenario around the hills indicated that they were getting close. The roads were smooth, but slant. Sam slowed down, partly because of the hilly tracks, and partly to absorb as much of the environment as he could.

"So?" Paridhi opened her eyes slowly. "Who are we visiting first?"

"Oh, you are awake?" Sam exclaimed. "You just missed the breathtaking view behind."

"I will see it when we return. You didn't answer my question."

"Radhika, of course," Sam spoke hurriedly "Ritesh has never been one of my favourites anyway."

"Hey, take it easy on him. Marriage resurrects the gentleman within most of the dummies that men are."

"That's very flattering," Sam smiled in sarcasm.

"It doesn't apply to you, of course," she rubbed her hand to his face. "You are a sweetheart."

Sam relaxed his grip on the steering as breath seemed to leave his body in a rush. Paridhi's lips touched his cheek, and pressed on as both of them closed their eyes in ecstasy.

"Hands on the steering, please," Paridhi said, as she guided Sam's lost hands back to the car's controls.

Sam looked into her big, sparkling eyes. She flushed with shyness and slipped her head on his shoulder. Her body hugged his side, and she wrapped both her arms around his neck.

"Keep driving," she quietly whispered.

The next person to hug Sam was Radhika. She was sitting in the changing room, with wet *mehendi* on her hands when somebody came and told her that Samved had arrived. She had sprung out of her room barefooted, clad in a blouse and *lehenga*, and pounced on him, first thing.

"So you are Ritesh's bride?" Sam quipped. "He is one lucky bastard."

"Shut up," she punched him with a grin. "So, what's going on, busy guy?"

Paridhi had been standing near the car all this time. But the mention of the word busy made her giggle, and she was instantly spotted by Radhika. She looked at Paridhi with surprise. Nobody was accustomed to seeing Sam with a girl, Radhika being an exception to the case.

"Oh, hi," Paridhi shuffled nervously. "I am Paridhi."

"Shit." The shock on Radhika's face was too genuine to be true. "*She* is Paridhi? She is *that* Paridhi?"

The moment of silence that followed was awkward for all three of them. It seemed to hang on for a while, and lapsed. "Yes and no," Paridhi said, biting her lips, and shrugged. Everybody laughed.

"Samved talks a lot about you," Radhika would explain later. "He had this huge crush on you since he spotted you in his campus in his MBA days."

"Damn," Paridhi covered her face. "That explains a lot of things."

Sam looked here and there, trying to hide his embarrassment. Radhika grabbed his cheeks and shook his face.

"He is our sweetheart," she winked.

"I used the very same word for him, and quite recently," Paridhi laughed, seeing Sam blush and turn red.

"Oh God," Radhika leaned over Sam, doubled up in laughter. "I am so happy to see you again that I almost forgot that I am the bride here."

Her grave expression made Sam a little uneasy.

"I am getting married tomorrow." she said, making a sad face. "And I look like a ghost."

Sam started laughing, much to the dismay of the girls present in the room. "Trust me when I say this," he said to himself more than anyone else, "but from what I have seen lately, looking like a ghost would be a compliment to most girls as far as I am concerned."

Shruti twitched a little. Nobody could see her, not even Sam (without his crazy goggles), but she hid her face in her hands. Living or dead, a girl is a girl after all.

"Okay, nobody got the joke," Sam said apologetically. "Naturally."

"He has this dreadful habit," Radhika said, shaking her head. "Cracking these unintelligible, scientific jokes. When we were young, my parents started believing that I had gone mad or something, all because of him."

"What?" Paridhi looked genuinely baffled. "Why?"

"Because," Radhika said, "I used to burst into laughter, all of a sudden, on the dining table. This dog would crack a joke in the morning and I would finally understand the meaning at dinner time."

Sam was irritated.

"Okay, no more kidding," Radhika immediately course corrected. "Don't get angry at me, or you will spoil my wedding."

Sam's anger was instantly washed away by Radhika's words. She had this power to lift anybody's mood, and nobody knew how she did it. The only person who shared this talent was Ritesh, and even he got away with most of his offences due to his cheeky and innovative one-liners. A perfect match indeed! Sam, being the brightest and most matured person in his circle, knew this from the very beginning. For others, Ritesh and Radhika were two best friends who were supposed to be best friends only, but who would know better?

"There you go," it was Paridhi who interrupted his train of thoughts this time. "Lost in some thoughts again."

"You will get used to it someday," Radhika said, shaking her head. "Alright, now get a move on. You guys must be tired. Get a shower, and some rest. You have to help me out with a lot of things, especially you Paridhi. Everything's a mess here. My wedding is going to be a disaster."

"Yet it is the post-wedding scenario that I fear," Sam had learnt a lot from cheeky Ritesh, and even more from his recent adventures with Shruti.

"If I hadn't been so happy today," Radhika said with a smile, "you would have been dead before you said this."

"I so hate this word," Shruti said as soon as Sam found a moment to put his glasses on afterwards.. "Dead."

"What is with you?" Sam squealed at her. "You have been in a bad mood for, I don't know, a week? What has happened to you?"

"You won't understand."

"Stop doing that girl thing," Sam got up. "Tell me."

"I don't want to be like this," Shruti screamed at a barely audible volume. "I don't want to be in this form."

"Hey," Sam would have put his hands on her shoulders, but realized that it was futile. "Let's take it this way. We are two of a kind. There has never been a man whose best friend was a ghost. And better, we will always be there for each other."

"It is a nice way to put it, but you don't realize one thing. One day you will get married too. What next? You will get busy with your life, like you have been busy with Paridhi since last Thursday."

"Excuse me! One, you are the reason that I'm this close to Paridhi. Two, five days doesn't mean I don't have time for you. And lastly, nobody can actually separate the two of us. Even if I tell Paridhi about you, she wouldn't get jealous or insecure."

"Who are you talking to?" Paridhi's voice filled the room like water. Sam's glasses were designed to amplify the tiniest of sounds and optimize them for normal hearing, but sometimes they failed to manipulate normal sounds instantly. By the time his glasses adjusted to Paridhi's voice, his eardrums were already on the verge of collapsing. He removed the goggles and put them aside.

"You look cool in these," she said in a shaky voice. "But you don't need to wear them all the time."

"Are you okay?" Sam's question was triggered more by the urge to change the topic rather than genuine care. "You sound a little flustered."

"I am a little sick. I caught cold."

"You took something?" Sam looked at her with worry. "Thankfully, Radhika is a doctor too."

"She is a trauma surgeon, genius," she chided him playfully. "And again, you changed the topic without answering me. What were you doing in here?"

"I was practicing," Sam went babbling before he could think.

"You were practicing, for what?"

"I developed an interest in theatre arts recently. So I was just practicing dialogues from a famous play. I keep forgetting its name. It's right on the tip of my tongue."

Sam threw a bluff at her, and she bought it. She drew a long breath, and put her hand on his shoulder. "You and your hobbies."

When she left, Sam bolted the door and slumped into the bed. He couldn't risk letting Shruti's existence in anybody's knowledge, not yet. He needed some solid facts about the dead before he showed them to the world. Their interaction with the living would open up many new possibilities. Imagine a dead person testifying as a witness in his own murder case. It would be a revolution, but there were many challenges. The human race knew nothing about their deceased, and the unknown must be treated as a threat at all times. Peaceful ignorance, at the moment, seemed to be the most logical thing. Interaction would be thought of later, when the elusive afterlife would be demystified.

Shruti noticed the wrinkles on his forehead. She waited patiently for him to wear his glasses.

"Listen," Sam spoke up before Shruti could even begin to open her mouth. "I need you to tell me a few things about the dead. Tell me everything that you know."

"Hey, I think we agreed on this…"

"I remember that, but I really need to know these things," Sam rushed with his words. "I invented a great thing, but I need a lot of information before I let our world get into contact with yours."

Shruti's flickering image appeared to solidify for a moment. She had been drawn into the conversation that she had wished to postpone forever. Her eyes skipped across the room, hoping that Sam would forget what he had just said, but he wouldn't.

"The first thing you need to know," she finally spoke up, "is this, that ghost and spirit are entirely different entities. A spirit is the entity that inhabits a body and gives life. All living people are basically body and spirit, but that is the part you already know. The interesting part comes when a person dies."

Sam was solemn. He was a very good listener, who would never interrupt a speaker, or even make a single sound when somebody spoke. He would just give a reassuring nod, and the speaker, satisfied that he was being heard, would continue. Still, this was too intriguing to be passed up quietly.

"What happens then?" He asked fervently. "How do they become ghosts?"

"The important question is that who all become ghosts?" Shruti's eyes were looking into some other plane. "Everybody doesn't. From all I have seen, I think there is one single criterion that decides whether a person becomes a ghost or not."

"What is that?"

"It is the same thing that attracts the lot of us; strong, unquenched emotions. They seem to be linked to a spirit's energy profile somehow. Emotions, like spirits, are a form of energy, rather than chemical secretions as we have always believed. I don't know where they come from or what provides that energy to a spirit. All I know is this that this surge of energy decides whether a spirit is able to cross over or not."

"Cross over, where?" Sam was getting more confused with each sentence Shruti said.

"I read some mythology to understand human-ghost interactions that have happened in the past. Many ancient civilizations believed that a spirit, after leaving the body, goes for its judgment. All those civilizations used the same term for the entity that makes the judgment, the bookkeeper. They believed that there were two worlds reserved for the living and the dead."

"So that was their equivalent of the mortal world and the world of the dead," Sam inferred. "But what happened to heaven and hell?"

"Now you are asking the right questions" Shruti chuckled, animated "There is no heaven or hell. It's just the living and the dead. But imagine what it would feel to be thrown out of place? What it would feel to be doomed to live in a world that is not your own, stuck for eternity? That's a ghost for you. And I believe it is reason enough for a spirit to become the malicious, murderous things they are generally thought to be."

Sam's eyes didn't betray the disgust and pity he felt, but his forehead wrinkled in despair. "What causes this suffering? Why would anybody be subjected to this torture? Is it their karma, their good or bad deeds?"

"I wish it were, Sam," Shruti withdrew in gloom. "I wish it were. But it isn't. There is no karma, no good or bad deeds, no virtues and evils. There is just one thing, and that is natural physics, cruel and logical."

"I don't...I don't...I don't understand." Shruti's hurt was getting reciprocated in Sam's voice. "What are you trying to say?"

"Let me explain this to you," Shruti whispered. "I have found that emotions are a form of radiant energy, nothing else. So, when you feel a lot of fear, or anger, or passion, or some other strong sentiment, your spirit loses a lot of energy. Can you follow me till here?"

Sam barely nodded, but Shruti wasn't waiting for his approval. She had picked her topic, and wouldn't stop until she was finished with it. "When you are alive, you have a lot of means of replenishing the energy you lose. When you feel angry, you lash out, but you cool down eventually. The fatigue goes away with time, doesn't it? Now, imagine that a person was in an emotionally charged state when he died. There is no means of getting that energy back."

"And that is the criterion you were talking about," Sam had comprehended the rest of her theory from what all he had heard. "Energy profile. Crossing over to the next world, whatever the name is, requires energy. That's pretty much like an electron jumping from one quantum state to another."

"You are not as dumb as I think," Shruti nodded appraisingly. "Dead right, you are!"

"So, that is how ghosts come into existence. Not meeting the energy requirement for the...*quantum* jump."

"The politically correct term is crossing over," Shruti intercepted. "The emotion that caused this energy drain, which forbade a spirit from crossing over, decides the nature of the ghost."

Sam's eyes reduced to minimum size. Shruti continued.

"See, there are many emotions that we experience. From all of these, only five are strong enough to forbid a spirit from a crossover. They are obsession, guilt, shock, dedication and revenge. Based on the particular emotion that the spirit cultivated at the time of death, a ghost can fall in one of five categories."

A laugh escaped from Sam's vocals. He felt guilty for laughing at such a grave issue, then drove the feeling away. If he, by any chance, died that very moment, this one emotion could turn him into a ghost. And that would be the very last thing he'd want.

"I see you've done your homework," he said, trying to cover up his thoughts. "Now, would you care to elaborate these *categories* of ghosts?"

"All in a day's work," she sighed and spoke simultaneously. "Okay. Let's begin with obsession. For an example, let me take you and Paridhi. You love her with a lot of passion, and you have waited for her for so long. Now if, God forbid, you die just after she rejected your love; you will become a ghost. You have an obsession for her, which will weaken your spirit if it goes unfulfilled."

Sam looked at Shruti with a blank face. Guilt or no guilt, he was destined to become a ghost.

"Come on, take it easy," Shruti said, having discovered his bafflement. "It won't happen with you. I am with you, so relax! Now, let me tell you about the other categories. We have guilty ghosts, who were hiding some crime when they died, or those who knowingly hurt the feelings of someone they loved. The ghosts of shock are those who died in an accident or a surprise assault. Ghosts of dedication are people who died fighting for or defending a cause or person or even the country. Lastly, we have ghosts of revenge. They are ghosts who died with a feeling of loss and injustice, and the futile urge to get even."

Sam took his time to process what he had just heard. He kept nodding for a couple of minutes.

"Okay I get it," he got up hurriedly. "I have just one last question. Which kind of ghost are you?"

Shruti smiled and giggled.

"I am what you can call a hybrid ghost. I belong to the first three categories."

Before Sam could express his surprise and confusion, Shruti interrupted him.

"I will explain this later. Somebody's coming."

She vanished with the knock on the door that followed. Sam removed his glasses and walked towards the door, but his attention was captured by suspense and wonder. The world around him was much more complicated than he, or anybody, knew.

The Proposal

The door opened to reveal a very baffled Sam inside. Radhika found it a little strange. Although, everybody knew Sam had this habit of getting lost in his thoughts and carrying the most alarming expressions, but he still wasn't supposed to behave like this all the time.

"What happened, Miss Gloom?" Radhika ruffled his hair. "At least *try* to look happy."

"I *am* happy," he jerked her hand off, absentmindedly. "Maybe it's my face that is not displaying it properly."

Radhika shook her head and dragged Sam away. She led him to her room, where Paridhi had slipped into one of Radhika's dresses. A purple one-piece paired with high heels. Sam stopped breathing for a while, but then realized that the world included a lot more than him and Paridhi. "You look stunning." For all his alertness, he couldn't stop those words from escaping his lips.

"Thank you," Radhika chuckled, holding Paridhi. "My dresses are always the best, and the girl in it is not bad either." Paridhi shuffled about, letting Sam see her from different perspectives.

Sam tilted his head, amused. He was with two of the most important people in his life, yet the room seemed empty without Shruti. He knew he was developing something for her, but couldn't figure out what it was. If it was friendship, it should've been more casual and sensible. She was out of his sight for less than five minutes, and he was missing her already. If it was...but it couldn't be. What about Paridhi? He had dreamed of her all his life, and now he was so close to having her. It would be stupid to think of anybody else presently, his mind said, especially when that someone belongs to another world. He whisked his thoughts away, labelling them as guilt pangs. *Guilt can make you a ghost.*

The next thing that transpired in his mind was a shrill scream from Radhika. It was a follow-up, actually. The triggering element was a car horn. Strange, who would be visiting them at midnight, approximately? His watch displayed 11:59 pm.

"It is Ritesh," Radhika answered Sam's doubt, almost hiding behind Paridhi. "But I can't meet him today. It's our wedding tomorrow."

"Not tomorrow," Sam corrected her, looking at his watch again. "Technically, it is today in...3...2...now."

Nobody was interested in Sam's perfectionist antics. Paridhi and Radhika scurried past him. Radhika almost lunged into the room straight ahead, and Paridhi scampered with the door. It closed from inside with a satisfying clink, and she eased her head on it.

"Samved, is that you?" Ritesh's husky voice cracked in excitement as he saw Sam.

"Who else did you expect?" Sam smiled a little, and hugged Ritesh.

"I wish Tina was here, I mean, the hug would have been more interesting. But not bad to see you either."

Ritesh. Tall. Fair. Playboy. Nothing seemed to have changed. "Still the bitch you always were," Sam's friendly rebuke would be taken as a compliment.

"Still the cry-baby you always were." Ritesh slipped a hand on Sam's shoulders, fluttering like a butterfly in a jar. For all his cool-dude antics, he was a man about to get courted. Nervousness was imminent.

Paridhi emerged from the curtain cover and froze, a little startled. Sam couldn't understand this reaction, for he had told her about Ritesh already. Then his look shifted sideways, and he understood. Ritesh was smiling so broadly at Paridhi, anybody would get uncomfortable. Paridhi knew about Ritesh, not the other way round.

"Wow, I mean hi," Ritesh blurted. "I don't remember if we have met, but I find your face quite familiar."

"I can assure you this," Sam caught Ritesh's arm to stop him from advancing. "You haven't met her before, ever."

"You seem to know her well enough, obviously." Ritesh dipped his razor-sharp comment in hot sarcasm and drove it straight into poor Sam. "Your track-record with girls has been quite a tale."

Sam suppressed the instant urge to smack Ritesh's head off the socket. Ritesh had all the good intentions in the world, but he had no idea how much his smartass talk infuriated people.

Nobody confronted him about it, though. It was nearly impossible to beat him in an argument or to make him accept the flaws of his attitude. So, all the genuineness he got was behind-the-back. That's where Radhika came in. She appeared to be a simple girl to most people, but only a select few knew that it was just a poster image of her true personality. Inside, Radhika was a control freak, who was all out passion in everything. Ritesh followed a very basic maxim in life, which he called fight-and-forget. He never dragged his fights. But Radhika didn't consider sparing as an option. If somebody crossed Ritesh, he could get a white flag from him, but Radhika never forgave such a person. She had been equally defensive for Sam as well, but in case of Ritesh, her impulsiveness became too obvious.

"Actually," Paridhi's voice broke Sam's chain of thoughts. "He is the only one in this house who knows me well enough."

Ritesh's lips twisted in a bizarre smile. "Miracle of miracles," he said, patting Sam. "So she is *your* friend?"

"Girlfriend."

The following moments were about people looking at each other in orderly patterns. Sam was staring at Paridhi, Paridhi was staring at Ritesh, and Ritesh was shifting his glance from Paridhi to Sam, and then back again.

"I AM GOING TO KILL YOU, Samved SINGH," Radhika jumped out of her room shouting, and then paused with a whimper as she saw Ritesh.

"Hi honey," Ritesh smiled awkwardly. "I missed you a lot."

The reaction was a quick squeak from Radhika, followed by a loud thud of the door as she hid herself in her room again. Ritesh looked around, feigning genuine surprise. "Did I do something?"

"Let me see," Sam put his fingers to his brows. "You turned up a tad too early for your wedding, without the crowd, I must add. Then, you saw Radhika, when you are clearly forbidden to do so. Considering the fact that you are Ritesh Chahal and you and rules don't really gel, I guess that there is nothing we should worry about. It's more or less routine stuff."

Ritesh stood gaping at Sam. He had never expected him to speak more than twenty syllables at a time. Sam was a nerd, and this sudden surge of wits was unprecedented. He turned to face Paridhi. "What have you been feeding him?"

"Jet-fuel," Sam snapped. "Keeps me swift."

"Oh man," Ritesh sighed and his eyes lit up. "This is awesome. You have started to sound like me, dude."

"I think we should look out for Radhika," Paridhi suggested, and guided Ritesh to the guest room.

"You can't stay here, idiot," Radhika was chiding Ritesh. "Dad is coming in the morning, and mom has already landed in Dun. She can crash in anytime now."

"Relax darling," Ritesh smoothly set his hand on Radhika's shoulder. "I am not afraid of your father, and your mother admires me too much to be a threat."

"On your wedding day, everything seems to be a threat," Radhika muttered loudly.

"You have been watching too much T.V," Sam commented, much to Ritesh's glee.

"Finally, he said something I can agree with."

"Paridhi, please take your boyfriend out of the room," Radhika coolly spoke, looking towards the wall. "Me and my fiancée need to talk for awhile."

"What did I do now," Sam spread his arms indignantly.

The look on Radhika's face did not change. Everybody who knew her knew the fact that she had divine control over her expressions, facial, tonal, everything. If it hadn't been for her affinity for morality, she would've gained a name for duping the most vary. Ritesh also had these qualities, so he was one of the few people who could interpret her. Presently, she was amused to see Ritesh and happy for Sam, but she had to show them some wrath too. Ritesh should've had some patience and Sam should've told her about Paridhi.

"What wrong can you do," she smiled her stock plaster smile at Sam, who was intimidated instantly. "You were busy in work, you were busy with Paridhi, and you had loads of other things to do. Why would you trouble yourself with picking up your phone, calling your best friend in the motherfucking universe, and telling her about your life? Do you even remember your best friends and family anymore? Tell me, did you call your mom to my wedding?"

Sam lost his consciousness for a split second. He had forgotten to call mom. It didn't matter if somebody had sent the invitation or not. He was good as dead now.

"Dude, I will have a great time when she arrives here," Ritesh smiled slyly. Radhika glared at him vehemently, which turned him quiet instantly.

"I didn't expect this from you," Radhika frowned childishly. "I don't know what to say now. You didn't tell *me* about your relationship."

"*I* didn't know about it either," Sam replied loudly. "I am as surprised as you are."

"Okay, I am clueless here," Ritesh spoke up. "Fine, you got a girlfriend, and she is hot by the way. Neither of those things make sense to me. But, what do you mean when you say you didn't know about it? Is that even possible? You did what, proposed her and forgot about it?"

Everybody was staring at Paridhi now.

"Okay, I liked him for a long time, but he is my boss. How could I just tell him? Then we came here, and Radhika told me that he liked me too. So, when Ritesh tried to insult him, I couldn't control myself."

Everybody was still staring, but at Ritesh this time.

"You tried to insult my best friend," Radhika's voice was ice-cold, complimenting her wicked smile all too well. She picked up her sandals, brandishing them at Ritesh, who cowered slowly.

"Well, he is my friend too," he got up, followed by Radhika, and ran into the hall. Sam and Paridhi didn't bother to go and see the chase. They had each other to attend to, first.

Paridhi stepped in a little, looking into Sam's eyes constantly. He smiled at her, which was more of a concealed giggle, to be precise. He was having a moment, yes, but Shruti must've been having a great time watching everything.

"You look great today," he whispered, failing to marshal any thoughts. "Like, really great."

"So, shall I take it as a yes," Paridhi whispered back.

"What are you talking about?"

"I just proposed to you, back there when I said I am your girlfriend. What do you think?"

Sam's smile turned more plastic. He had imagined this moment all these years, yet now he was confused when it finally arrived.

"I guess I will have to think about it," he finally said, nodding his head and smiling and shrugging.

"Oh really," Paridhi grinned in amusement. "Shall I give you a deadline for that too?"

"I thought I was your boss."

"Well that's all justified," Paridhi closed in some more, half stepping on Sam's feet, holding his arms. "You are my boss in the office; I will be your boss at home. I handle everything for you at work; you will handle everything at home. That includes the laundry, the kitchen, and the future kids."

"I am a very bad cook," Sam exclaimed, trying to control his joy.

"So am I," Paridhi breathed, and pressed her moist lips against his. His hands deftly moved to her waist and collected all of her body as close as they could. She slacked up, resting completely in his arms. Sam took over from there, frantically caressing her, lips locked securely. Her velvet hands dug into his hair as waves of ecstasy filled her up. Meanwhile, some movement happened outside, but they could never care less. They drew away from each other very slowly, letting the impression and taste of their lips leaves an after effect. Paridhi held Sam's hands tightly, and then let her head rest on his shoulder, and he stroked her tresses gently. She couldn't stay that way however, as they had to step aside in the wake of their new visitors.

"And there is your culprit," Ritesh's voice broke in even before he entered the room, followed by his bride. Sam's mom entered next, her lips a wiry line and her brows propped up. She dismissed the presence of her son with a shrug and addressed Paridhi.

"I suppose we all have a wedding to attend today. So, it is better that we get some well-deserved sleep, isn't it?"

"I will take your luggage to your room," Paridhi nodded, and left hurriedly with the old lady in tow.

Sam rubbed his hands, searching for words. He turned to Ritesh. "You've got to talk to mom."

"On your behalf? Not happening, bro. She'll hack me into little pieces and feed me to my own wedding guests."

Sam looked at Radhika, who looked away. "She's my ad hoc mother-in-law now," she said. "She will think it well within her rights to serve me as sauce."

"Very tasty sauce," Ritesh quipped. Both Sam and Radhika smacked him across his head. "Not the time for this? Well, okay."

Leaving Early

"So why do you have different surnames when you are brothers?" Paridhi had found Sam after much difficulty inside Ritesh's bedroom, the latter being taken up with preparations. She figured that would be the best time to have a few moments alone with him. People had been pouring in all day, bringing all kinds of ancient wisdom on the subtle art of conducting a memorable wedding.

"We aren't brothers," Sam said. "Ritesh's mother was my mom's best friend. Single mother. She passed away when were twelve, a year before the accident that took my father. Since then, Ritesh became a part of my family. My mom took care of him until college, from there he became self-sustained."

Paridhi sat down on the bed, pulling him aside. "I'm sorry to hear about them. Why did Ritesh's relatives not take him in?"

"He had no relatives to do that," Sam looked the other way. "His mother's relatives disowned her because she married out of her caste. As for his father, he had no family to begin with. All we know is that he just took off when she got pregnant with Ritesh."

"Fucking animal."

Sam took a deep breath and nodded. "I think so too."

"You never told me about your father, though."

What's there to tell? He lived. He died. I loved him. There's nothing about this story that you haven't heard before."

"I know I'm being a little too intrusive here, Samved, but you can share these things with me." Paridhi paused. "If you want to."

"He died less than a hundred metres away from his home, our home," Sam's eyes focussed on the floor next to his feet, his lips curved tightly. "He was driving to home with my mother, like he had done hundreds of times before. He was the safest driver, ever. Always had two helmets with him, one for himself and one for the pillion rider. Respected speed limits. Nobody had seen him cross a 50, maybe 60 on a highway." He tensed up, his breathing turning into huffing. Paridhi placed her hands on his shoulders. "But when the day comes the day comes, I suppose. A dog came in his way. A little white street dog. It is unclear what exactly happened. There were barely any scratches on their helmets. His bike had zero damage. Zero damage. I remember one day the bike fell when I was trying to put it on the main stand and broke the indicator light. Not that day, though. Zero fucking damage. The accident happened at no more than the speed of 40. But they died. The only good news is that, while he died, he saved that dog."

Sam bit his lower lip until it bled. Paridhi clutched his shoulders tighter. "That's how Radhika's dad clutched my arm that night," he turned to face her, pearl of tears forming around the corners of his eyes. "I was near the ICCU. I asked the nurse where my father was and when could we see him. Uncle clutched my arm. I asked again. His grip tightened. I asked again. He kept squeezing my arm tighter and tighter. That was when I knew it. But I kept asking. I had to hear it. I had to make it real. So I asked again, and he held my hand just as tight as you are holding my shoulders right now and he said 'you don't have a father anymore'."

Paridhi's head was dug in his chest, her tears falling inside his shirt. Between laboured breaths, she said "you can cry, Sam. You can let it out."

"I can't cry," Sam looked up. "I didn't get that chance. Mom was hurt due to that accident, so we couldn't tell her or she would refuse first-aid. Considering that, I had to hide the fact that dad had gone. The rest of dad's friends and relatives were doing the same thing. The ladies would come crying, but they were silenced by the men. Only the most calm ones were allowed to enter the hospital reception where mom was. The rest were made to wait outside. Me, I just kept lying. 'The doctors are working', 'they are still diagnosing', 'they will tell us something as soon as they finish some tests', I kept producing more lies. When mom went in to get her wounds cleaned and dressed, they took dad's body out and we got him into the mortuary. Afterwards, when I did tell mom the truth, there was too much wailing. The women were screaming. I don't know, I couldn't cry. Maybe because I thought that I had to put up a brave front. Maybe because all the screaming and the wailing made it impossible to concentrate on crying. Maybe because when they said that it was god's will I felt so much rage that it burned the tears inside of my eyes. I just know that I couldn't cry for the next 13 days. And even after that, mom did enough crying for two people. Now, there's just no point."

Paridhi was shaking. She gulped air to calm down. "Still," she said, "it is better to cry and get your emotions out of your system." She wrapped her arms around Sam, whose tears had finally left his eyes.

"After keeping it in for so long," he said, "it is much harder to let it out."

Shruti was having a fun day. It had been a long time since she had seen a wedding. After her demise, she had become too depressed and dull to take interest in human matters. She used to roam around aimlessly, thinking about the mistakes of her life, until Sam came and changed all of it. First he gave her a chance to help him to get his love requited, and then he became her best and only friend. She had started seeing the world with a different perspective. Death had brought a lot of drawbacks, but the possibilities it offered were endless. She had kept herself busy all day pulling gigs at the guests and freaking them out. In the morning she possessed a young woman who had come to attend the wedding with her mother, and made her do all kinds of crazy stuff. The girl's mother got quite a scare. Then she started doing all sorts of ghost publicity stunts, which spooked out even the most sceptic guests. Sam had been noticing this, so she kept her antics down to a barely perceptible level. She had always been the rebellious kind, so she had a habit of going reckless now and then. Still, the day passed slowly and she felt bored as she couldn't talk to Sam. Most of her time was spent wandering around Radhika, who was being groomed beyond earthly limits.

In the evening, the groom arrived with a bunch of young guns suited up and ready to dance their butts off. Some of them were quite dashing; too bad that they were beyond reach for poor Shruti. Ritesh certainly looked his best, dressed charmingly for the occasion. He wore a cream sherwani, and footwear that Sam had gifted him for the wedding. Sam wasn't dressed badly either, he was in a nice and comfy ensemble Paridhi had selected for him. He had requested her to wear a sari on the wedding, and as she wasn't quite used to Indian outfits, it took a lot of persuasion before she agreed on it. Both of them got busy entertaining the new guests while Radhika and the other ladies went to fetch Radhika. The guests instantly hurled themselves at the food. That's the thing about Indian weddings; most of the guests behave as if they were starved for quite a long time before they finally arrived at the party. Paridhi never left Sam's side, and they were seen holding hands most of the time. Meanwhile, Ritesh looked quite restless as he waited for his bride.

Radhika made her appearance after an entire hour (generally, it's the groom who makes people wait). Ritesh had almost bitten his nails off, and Sam had almost begun to worry. Anyways, a wave of excitement enveloped the guests when she came. The crowd clapped and cheered quite loudly as Radhika took her place near the altar, next to her soul mate. They passed a soft smile to each other, a seemingly childish smile, which actually was an entire conversation encrypted and compressed into a simple twist of the lips. Radhika noticed that Ritesh's legs were shaking, and she nudged Paridhi, who in turn drew Sam's attention at it. While everybody watched, yet nearly nobody really did, Radhika's hand slipped over Ritesh's knee, and the tremors in his body and in his heart eased out. Ritesh placed his hand over hers, and they exchanged another wee smile.

"Hold the horses, lovers," Sam quipped. "You don't have the license to do all this yet."

Everybody started laughing, making Radhika blush very prominently, but that wasn't the interesting part. For the first time ever, Ritesh Chahal was blushing. Meanwhile, the laughter smoothed out, only to be roused again.

"Look who's talking," Radhika addressed Sam, and the grin on her face made it clear what she was up to. "You are asking our bride and groom to hold their horses. What about the stuff you've been doing with Paridhi all day?"

This time the joke was on Sam. Ritesh and Radhika leaned over each other, bent in laughter. Radhika chuckled as if she had won an Oscar or something. Luckily, Sam's mom interrupted the fun and asked the pundit to begin with the rituals.

Sam felt a soft, warm sensation slide between his fingers. A tight clasp followed, and he looked down to discover that it was Paridhi holding his hand. He pressed back at her soft wrist, and her slender body melted against his solid frame as she rested her head on his shoulder and let go of his hand in order to hold his arm. He slipped his hand across her bare waist but didn't pull her any closer, thanks to the crowd surrounding them. Her breaths splashed across his face occasionally, but both of them controlled themselves and concentrated on the wedding rites.

"Well," Paridhi would sigh later, "it went well, I suppose."

"I can't believe they have finally got married," Sam added.

Paridhi gazed at him intently as he described his own thoughts and concerns about the two. Sam didn't care much about Ritesh, although he tried his best to do so. While Paridhi had no idea what the fuss was, she knew that Sam was deeply disturbed by it; so she didn't ask him anything. Radhika, on the other hand, was a different story entirely. Sam had been her guardian angel since childhood, and she had been the same to him. These two weren't the textbook definition of best friends but they always knew the important stuff about each other. Paridhi felt good for no reason, maybe it was because of the way he described Radhika and his friendship with her. If a man had so much heart for his friend, one could be sure that his life partner would get utter bliss.

"I see that you have acquired Radhika's staring habit," Sam snapped his fingers to bring Paridhi out of her trance.

"No, but if you see what I see, you will stare too," she riddled Sam into confusion and stepped forward and kissed him. They couldn't relish the moment, though, as Paridhi suddenly reeled away.

Sam held her arms. "Are you okay?"

"He can see me."

"Who can what?"

Paridhi shrugged and released herself, and pointed towards the corridor that led down to the sprawling lawn where the wedding after-party was still going on.

"Your friend, Ritesh," she whispered. "He can see me."

Sam looked at her weirdly. He was a little surprised to see Paridhi behave like this.

"It is okay," he cackled nervously. "He looks at every girl like that."

Paridhi smacked him right across his head with a disgusted frown. "You idiot, stupid moron," she let out a suppressed scream. "It is me, Shruti."

Sam gaped like never before.

"You possessed my girlfriend?" He snorted. "And just a minute. How can Ritesh see you? Even I can't see you right now!"

"I don't know," she squealed and moved around in panic. "I have no idea how that is possible, but I know he can see me. When he first arrived, and all you people were talking, he would look at me again and again. He even tried to gesture something at me. It was as if he knew I was there and he wanted me to stay away."

"It isn't possible," Sam held her by the arms again. "He can't see you. Maybe he was just looking around as all of us do."

"Are you out of your mind?" Shruti jerked him away; again. "Do you think I would panic so much if that was a possibility? I am a ghost, I see and feel everything. I know when people are looking and when they are just looking around. I don't know if he is some kind of psychic or clairvoyant, but he can see me. And I don't think he likes me."

"If that is true," Sam replied after a long pause, "what are we going to do about it?"

"I am leaving this place," Shruti declared huskily. "I will see you back at home. Have fun with Paridhi and your friends, and take care of yourself. I won't be around, so don't do anything reckless or stupid."

"What the hell?" Sam complained. "It's you who does the reckless and stupid stuff, not me."

"What? Wait! Did I just say something? I think I blacked out for a moment." And Paridhi was back with him. *'I hate ghosts!'* - Sam thought to himself.

"It's okay dear," Sam caressed her warm face and held her hands. "You need to get some sleep. You have been up and working without getting proper sleeps for quite a while now."

"I don't feel tired or sleepy," she said. "I just had a moment of lapse, I don't know how."

"You don't feel tired but you are. And our newlywed bride is a doctor. So before she comes to know about this and starts making a prescription, you'd better do as I tell you."

"Okay boss, I'm all yours," she grinned.

Sam took her to his mom's room, which was the only room that hadn't got overcrowded with gifts and clothes and other stuff. Although Paridhi didn't feel so, she actually was quite tired. She fell asleep as soon as she hit the bed, part of her anyway. She was practically sleeping in Sam's arms, so he lay down for a while as well. As he untangled the stray locks of her hair and caressed her tender body, he closed his eyes to record the memory forever. He had dreamt of this for years. He was with the girl he loved, and she was cuddled to him, warm and peaceful. It was as if he was wrapped in a velvet blanket, breathing and heaving. She murmured something unintelligible in her sleep, and then a gust of her hot, sweet-scented breath seeped through his shirt. She shivered as the night's coldness glided over her prone body, clad in a thin little sari. Sam covered her in a quilt and stayed stuck with her until she was completely warm. Then he tucked her in, safe from the icy arms of Dehradun winter and left to look after the wedding party going on in the lawn. It was half past ten, the party hadn't even begun.

"There he is." Radhika nearly screamed when Sam appeared near the dais, where people had been crowding around to get photographed with the just married couple. They had left quite a while earlier, leaving the stage empty save for Radhika and Sam's mom, who had been with Radhika and Ritesh all the time.

"Where were you, you stupid moron?" Radhika was indignant. "You missed all the fun."

"Really" He smiled. "I did? No problems, you will tell me anyway. Paridhi was tired and a little spent out. You know, she doesn't have much tolerance for cold. So I put her to bed."

"Don't tell me," Ritesh dropped in. "You put her to bed, and came back? I mean, you had the girl and you had the bed. And you came back? Grow up sissy."

Radhika nudged Ritesh in embarrassment while Sam's mom gave him a high-five. "Mr. Ritesh Chahal," Radhika's tongue struck like a steel whip dipped in magma hot, molten sarcasm. "You are not going to get either of the two - the girl or the bed - tonight. I am postponing our first night."

Ritesh's face drooped like a snowman under the sun. Radhika and Sam bent and leaned over each other, laughing. "First week of your married life and you get grounded," Sam borrowed some sarcasm from Radhika's dungeon. "Grow up sissy." Radhika high-fived again but this time it was Sam.

"I don't like this guy anymore," Ritesh shook his head. "Man, he is becoming better than me."

"Ma'am, please gather around close to each other for the photo," a voice strayed into their circle. All of them noticed the camera, and struck a nice pose. While Radhika was all happy and satisfied, Sam was a little worried about Paridhi who was safely asleep. Ritesh was congratulating himself for a successful wedding. One photo said many different things that night.

Revelation

A warm light descended upon the chilled, shaking Dehradun. Nobody had expected a bright sunny morning after the night that had just passed. The heavy morning dew, which had added to everybody's misery, was also gone now. The beauty of the morning sun is best realized after a freezing cold night. Paridhi half-opened her eyes and smiled at the sun knocking at the window. The last thing she remembered was being put to sleep by Samved. Although she had fallen asleep very quickly in his warm embrace, but she remembered how the howling cold night had descended upon her and how Sam had stayed with her. She smiled again, savouring the fact that she had met the perfect man. Sam was everything a girl could ever wish for. She yawned and stretched herself a little. She was completely fine now.

As she turned, she spotted Radhika lying down right beside her, staring at her. "Good morning dear," she grinned. "I caught you smiling there. You were thinking about Samved, right?"

Paridhi took a long pause, so Radhika just went on. "Come on, don't be shy. I am his best friend. You can tell me anything."

"Yes, I was thinking about him," Paridhi smiled again. "He is not somebody you can get off your mind."

"Hmm, that's right," Radhika chuckled with a wink. "But don't tell him that. For all the shyness he shows, he is a big time attention-seeker."

"You should've told me this before I fell in love with him. Now I am a gone case. And I really am a person who spoils people."

Radhika shook her head with a bright eyed smirk, and hugged Paridhi. "Oh, you are such a sweetheart. I am so glad Samved got you. Now I will go and tell everybody that you passed the test."

"This was a test?"

"Of course this was a test. What did you think? I am Samved's best friend. You can't marry him without my approval. But never mind, I think you are just the girl for him."

Paridhi couldn't stop laughing. Sam was right. These people were not just friends, they were family. And they were the best people to have around.

Meanwhile Sam was helping his mother with cleaning up the house. They had their hands full too, because every inch of the house was filled with unnecessary items that had been brought in as wedding arrangements. The lawn was a horrible mess! And the chilly morning had not helped them much either. But as the sun came up and thawed Dehradun back to life, work became a lot more fun. Nevertheless, it took them an exhausting noon to finally get the house ready for the new couple. Ritesh and Radhika had been left not to be disturbed, but they spent the entire day snoring over each other. Radhika went in to ask them if they needed anything, but came back without a word. Everybody deserves a day off. Mom decided to let Sam and Paridhi have some time together as well, so she shifted to Radhika's room for the evening. Sam had a refreshing sleep in Paridhi's waiting arms after a hard day's work.

At night Paridhi left to help Radhika in the kitchen, although there wasn't much for her to do. Radhika and Ritesh were still locked up in their room. So, Sam decided to get sneaky and open up the presents. All of us have another side to our personality, the dark one (or the red one with the arrow-headed tail). In Sam's case, the other side was sneaky. And nobody would mind him either. He rummaged through the neatly stacked wedding presents in an almost watchful fashion, as if he was looking for something in particular. There were big boxes lavishly wrapped up in the most garish gift-wraps ever, and there were some classy looking presents which almost appeared to be transparent crystal all the way down. He didn't touch any of those. This was regular stuff, and Sam had no interest in the mundane. He always scavenged out the most peculiar looking gift out of the stockpiles, be it his birthday or somebody else's party. And there it was, almost hidden in the corner, a little cubical box sitting about like a small telephone booth in the Manhattan of huge wedding presents.

"Whoa, you got an interesting one here, Ritesh," Sam muttered to himself. He toyed with the box in his hand, looking at it very closely. The box was wooden, but not normal wood. It was scented wood, not sandal or anything he knew. Also, it had a very smooth, almost velvety finish, but it appeared to be very strong. What he found peculiar, though, was that the box had no opening. It was pretty much sealed, or maybe it wasn't a box at all. It appeared to be a solid block of wood, but it was certain that there was something inside it.

"Who gives away gifts like this?"

Sam kept fiddling with the box (or block), trying to figure out what it was. Then his eyes fell upon an inscription carved into the bottom face. Peculiar again, as he had examined the box like six times already but had never come across the lettering.

I drop a pebble into the river of time. I know not where the current might take it, but I hope a little boy discovers it downstream, and my name may exceed my life. With love

Your Father

Sam felt his muscles go numb and nearly dropped the box. He looked around, drenched in cold sweat. He got up slowly, and opened his bag and slipped the box inside.

"Come on Sam," Paridhi appeared at the door. "Dinner is ready."

"I'll be right there," Sam replied.

"Is everything okay? You seem to be a little worried."

"No I was just thinking that if you are feeling better now, we should leave tomorrow. We have a lot of work piled up."

"Don't worry baby. We are the best team ever. We will catch up with work and we'll still have enough time to make out in the office."

"Looks like I got a wild one here," Sam slid his arm around Paridhi's waist and pulled her in, and she caressed his hair.

"You do all the tugging, and I am the wild one?"

"Well you ask for it," Sam brushed his nose against hers. "You give me the signal. All I do is reacting to it."

"Oh, I give you the signal?" Paridhi cooed into his ears. "Bad move boss, trying to establish that a girl is desperate for you."

"Tell me if I am wrong."

"Absolutely not, I am desperate for you."

"No more talking then."

"No, wait," Paridhi stopped him. "Come and have dinner first. This we'll continue later."

"Why, what's wrong with now?"

"Nothing, I am just saving myself for dessert."

"I can't believe you just said that, you naughty girl."

Paridhi turned red, having realized that she had indeed behaved very desperately. She gave Sam a long kiss on his cheek, released herself, and walked away.

"So this was the appetizer, I suppose?"

The next morning, Sam and Paridhi were packed and ready to go.

"I will miss you dear," Radhika whispered as she embraced Sam.

Sam grinned at Ritesh. "I know. With this guy around, I am sure to be badly missed."

"Well, I got no reason to miss you," Ritesh grinned back. "But it's more fun to have you around rather than not."

Radhika just took Sam's hand, and put them in Paridhi's hands. "Take care of this stupid idiot for me. And if he ever hurts you or mistreats you, just tell me or his mom. We will fix him."

"I will miss you too," Sam said.

Radhika made a sulky face at him, and then smiled.

"I will meet you guys at your wedding. And this time, please don't forget to invite your mom."

The sun had just come up, flushed at the world bashfully for a while, and then came to its full glory. The mild mist still persisted, giving all of Dehradun a paradise-like feeling. The forest surrounding the place was strikingly green, soft on the eyes and cool to the mind. People who have been higher up into the mountains know what actual paradise looks like, but Sam and

Paridhi were two city folks who had never seen anything in their lives but the concrete jungle and the wild rush called metropolitan life. As rubber burned against the cold hard road, they looked around and tried to absorb as much of the hills as they could.

"After a few years," said Paridhi, "when we earn enough money and stability, I'd like to shift here. This neighbourhood is far better than our own."

"One day we will live here," Sam said.

When Sam said 'we', he meant him, Paridhi *and Shruti*.

"I see that you missed me," Shruti winked as soon as Sam put on his glasses, which was immediately after he entered his own bedroom in his own house.

"Oh, don't be so sure," Sam teased her.

"Yeah, but the first thing you do as soon as you enter the house is find your glasses and put them on. What else am I supposed to infer?"

"Nothing, I just have a lot of things to tell you. You ran away and left me alone."

"I left you *and Paridhi* alone," Shruti hovered around with a flicker. "You wouldn't want me watching when you pushed your tongue down her throat, among other things."

"Well, if I remember the details properly, you possessed my girlfriend right in the middle of our first kiss. So technically, I pushed my actual tongue down *your* proverbial throat."

"Oh, gross," Shruti grimaced. "In my defence - first, it was your second kiss. Second, it was necessary."

Sam brought a half-smile to his face and raised his eyebrows. "Okay, no one would argue with you. Did you miss me, though?"

"Of course I did. Anyways, how is Paridhi? And how are you two doing?"

Sam's eyes beamed his excitement, no matter how hard he tried to hide it. "We're going great. Although it's practically a three day old relationship, but it seems to be one that will stay."

"It will."

"Which brings me to this," Sam sat straighter and looked straight into her black eyes. "Why did you run away?"

"I've already told you."

"Now that," Sam nodded with a satirical look, "is really going to hurt my ego. I wasted so much time and energy to build this device that allows me to communicate with ghosts like yourself, and witty Ritesh can see you just like that? That man's really got his virtues right."

"If you don't want to believe me, don't. I don't need to justify myself either. I'll do whatever I like. I'll go right now if I choose to. Stop me if you can."

"Don't test me with your anger. I know how fake it is. Tell me the truth."

"I told you the truth," Shruti said, "and that's all you need to know."

"Is it now?"

"Look, Sam, please don't ask me too many questions already. You're just back. Take some rest. We will talk about this later."

"Don't tell me you cooked something fancy for me."

Shruti let out a happy sigh. "You're so funny," she smiled. "Trust me, I'd cook for you all my life if I could."

"And how long would that be? Twenty three years?"

"Twenty four years. I died sixteen days after my twenty-fourth birthday."

"Damn, you died young and ripe. What a poor, unlucky world this is."

"How many times do I have to ask you to not flirt with me? You are a committed man now." Shruti's eyes sparkled with humour. "Besides, I died seven years ago. I'd have been out of your reach anyway. Like, generation gap."

"Yeah, that's a point. I guess everything happens for a reason. Maybe you were always supposed to come and change my life."

"Yes, as you were supposed to change mine, Samved. Nobody's ever had a friendship like ours, and nobody ever will."

"I am sure of that," Sam said. "Anyways, there is something weird that I have to show you."

"Really," Shruti frowned. "I thought you were the last weird thing left."

"Oh, you've got no idea."

Sam opened his bag and produced the little box he had stolen from the pile of Ritesh and Radhika's wedding presents. "I found this the day after you left Radhika's wedding," he said. "Something tells me that you can find out what it is and how it reached there."

"Why don't you look at it yourself," said Shruti. "You have your glasses on. Right now, you can see what I can."

Sam stared at Shruti for a moment, and then at the box. She was right. He could see it now. The box appeared to be a shadow covering a bright little star. It looked like a purple sun shining through the foggy layers of the cold night. Sam's eyes spread out wide at the magnificent little marvel he was holding in his hand, totally unaware of its power.

"What is this thing?"

"I am not sure," Shruti said, "but it seems to be an ancient relic. There are a very few people who know about these things. I used to study these things, and those people."

"What do you mean?"

"For a normal person, this is just an antique. The only importance one would associate with this object would be either strictly monetary or historical. But people aware of ancient myth and occult know better. This is one of the very few objects that connect the other side with this world, an object that exists in both the physical world and the other world at the same time, and equally accessible at both sides too."

"I didn't understand a word of whatever you just said."

"I don't understand it either. Not completely at least. Anyways, let me show you. Give me the box."

Sam looked surprised but handed over the box to Shruti quite immediately. As he had expected, the box went right through her hand and dropped on the floor. But the purple ball of light didn't pass through her. It stayed there, rested on the top her palm. Shruti's eyes glowed with ecstasy as she felt the queer warmth spreading through her.

"You see?" Shruti said. "This is how it works. I can hold it, and so can you. Go ahead."

Sam outstretched his hand and grabbed one end of the little orb, the other end being stuck in Shruti's fingers. It was more of a ribbon than an orb, but the glow made it hard to determine the shape.

"Oh, this is awesome. I've never seen something like this in my entire life, and death." Shruti gaped at the wonder she was sharing with Sam.

Suddenly, something frightening happened. The purple ribbon snapped into two halves and melted. It raced up Sam and Shruti's hands like flowing mercury, and galvanized around their wrists in no time. Now they could identify the shape. The object had been a wristband, only now it had replicated. Sam had one over his wrist and Shruti had the other one. Shruti's face suddenly fell, causing Sam to panic too.

"What happened to you Shruti? Why do you look so upset?"

"I am not upset," she said. "I mean, this is amazing, but I am confused. Who gave this to Ritesh? And between him seeing me and this, I really think there is something with this guy that you don't know. There has to be something."

"You know, there is one thing that I don't understand. Why are you so afraid? You are a ghost; nobody can do anything to you."

"That's where you are wrong Sam," Shruti said. "I am afraid because there is a threat out there for me too. I am a ghost, and there are things that can do a lot to me."

"What do you mean?"

"Ghosts don't live forever Sam. If you die and you go to the other side, you simply come back and get reborn again and again. That's supposed to be the natural cycle of life. But if you become a ghost, you disturb the balance of nature. You become a chunk of energy that becomes unavailable to the cycle. Besides, ghosts suck energy from the system and become stronger and more dangerous. That's why there are creatures that nature appointed to terminate ghosts too."

"What? You are telling me that ghosts can be killed?"

"No, it's much worse. Ghosts can be destroyed. You see, my kind is the fraction of souls which got out of line. Normal souls retain their life force;

they live after and beyond death. But ghosts are destroyed. When we are killed, nothing remains. We just end."

"This is bullshit. How do you know that?"

"I know, because I've seen that happen. I've seen them, those things, killing people who had already died. What do you think; I was always this lonely sulky thing floating around with meaningless existence? No Sam, I didn't die when my body did. No matter how broken I felt, no matter how much I had left behind me, but I still lived. I found people of my kind, other ghosts. I found a new family. Then they came. The *enforcers* of nature came. They hunted us down and killed us, one at a time. We could do nothing. They'd come in large hordes and they would rip my brothers and sisters apart. The strongest of us fell before them like ninepins. And they never stopped, until they'd shred every piece of every ghost's existence and return the energy to nature."

She looked around in helpless remorse and continued.

"At last, only three of us were left. We were survivors. We never fought, never made a move. We just hid and ran, and we did that very well. But one day I screwed up, and the last of my friends died - no, got annihilated - trying to save me. Since then I just kept running, until you found me and gave me a third life. But now I think it's all going to end."

"Why do you think so? If you have eluded them so far, you can do that again. You can do that forever." Sam stared at her with hope, his eyes wet.

"You don't understand Sam. I don't want to run anymore. Running is no use. It's better to die and be remembered than to live and be forgotten."

"Now where did that come from?"

"You never asked me how these *enforcers* find their targets," Shruti interrupted him. "Let me tell you. We ghosts feed off the energy directed towards us. When people fear us or when we find peace, joy, love, we get stronger. And that's when we get caught. My friends died because they chose not to live lone, desolate lives. We chose to live together as a family. We loved each other, cared for each other, looked out for each other. That's what got us destroyed in the end."

"And now that you found me, you think that those hunters will find you? Trust me; they'll have to go through me to get to you."

"You can't fight them Sam. Nobody can fight them."

"I am a scientist. You have no idea what I can do."

"Just keep yourself safe and live a great life with Paridhi. That's all I want you to do."

"Shruti, this is stupidity. You should save yourself and run. That's why all those ghosts, friends of yours, died."

"They didn't die so that I could keep running. They died so that I could find a reason to stop running."

"What do you mean?"

"The strongest ghost in my family was Anasuya. She had been a ghost for eight hundred years when I met her. She was so strong that she actually destroyed a lot of *enforcer*s before she was taken down. She could make lightning strike with her power. When she found me, she said that she had found her lost sister. She said that she was sure that I had been her sister in my previous life. And she told me that she had been hiding and running so far only because she wanted to find me. All the ghosts in my family were in search of something or someone. When they found what they were looking for, they all happily accepted their fate. That's what I am doing now."

"So you found what you were looking for," Sam sighed. "What was that thing?"

"It was you Sam," Shruti looked into his eyes and opened her heart. "I was looking for you all along, but never quite saw you. I saw and I learnt a lot with you. I love you Sam, but you must let me go."

"Okay, you're free to go," a strong feminine voice entered Sam's bedroom in a straight flush. "In fact, if you don't leave in the next ten seconds, you're as good as dead."

Sam removed his glasses and looked behind. Paridhi was standing at the door, wearing a pretty angry look.

"What happened to you Paridhi," Sam asked. "And who were you talking to?"

"Get her out of here," Paridhi commanded.

"Get who out?"

"The girl who is sitting next to you on your bed," Paridhi said. "I think I deserve an explanation right now."

Answers

Sam stayed frozen for three complete seconds. His mind had already done the math, but he had no courage to turn his head and confirm the conclusion he had reached. Paridhi's infuriated demeanour didn't matter at the moment. The weirdest miracle had probably happened. Slowly, Sam turned to face Shruti, who looked no less surprised. He extended his hand to touch her. As he made contact with Shruti's smooth, warm skin, a tear escaped her eye and flowed right over his hand.

"This is impossible," said Sam. "You are alive."

"I can't believe it," Shruti jittered as ecstatic sobs overtook her and clasped Sam's hand tightly.

"What is going on here?" Paridhi broke in, taking Sam out of the trance.

"You wouldn't believe me if I told you."

"Fine," Paridhi retorted. "Then I will leave you two alone. Have fun."

She turned and started to march out of the room. But she just couldn't cross the doorway. It was as if somebody had made a glass screen across it. She placed her stretched palms over the invisible wall and struggled between the choices of fainting or facing what was to come next.

"Don't be afraid of us Paridhi," Shruti called out. "Nobody is going to harm you."

"What is going on here?" Paridhi was hysterical, but her voice remained soft and trembling.

"It is a long story dear," Sam held her hands and said. "Calm down, I will explain everything. Please sit down. I am right here."

Sam was right. It was a long story, and Paridhi had no idea what to believe at the end of it. Her mind fiddled with the idea of Sam being crazy, but there were too many weird things that would go unexplained. So she decided to trust her boyfriend and play along for the time being.

"So you made a device," she said, holding her head, "that can see ghosts. She was the ghost you found, and now she is a living human being. And I have to believe all of it?"

Shruti stretched her arm outwards forcefully. Instantly, the windows of the room were shattered as if someone with a giant fist had smashed them down. And four feet tall window panes of crown glass are not known to self-destruct in normal cases.

"I could blow the wall too, but it's going to be your house sooner or later; and it doesn't need renovation yet," she told Paridhi.

"Why couldn't you just make something hover and settle back down?" Sam muttered.

"This is unbelievable," Paridhi held her head between her hands. "What the hell is she? This is unbelievable."

"She is a friend," Sam held her hands again. "Relax now. I knew it would be hard for you to believe, that's why I didn't tell you about her."

"May I see your glasses?"

"Yes, sure you can. But I don't think you'll see anything special. It took me days to find Shruti."

Paridhi wasn't listening. She had always been an adventure loving girl full of curiosity, especially towards the paranormal. She still hadn't believed Sam completely, but she wanted to. She took the glasses and put them on.

"It's beautiful," she said. "I can see so many colours."

"Yes, I know," Sam sighed.

"Hey, why do you appear purple? Does this device show people in purple?"

Paridhi's question startled Sam and Shruti alike.

"No, it isn't supposed to do that," said Sam. "It doesn't add any colours from its own. It shows people as you'd see them without the glasses."

"Well, that's funny. You two appear as if paint-balled purple."

Paridhi got up and walked up to the broken window which overlooked the long alleyway. She looked around, rocked back in surprise, and removed the glasses. Her face lit up with a mesmeric smile, and she put the glasses back on.

"I think I see ghosts," she whispered in ecstasy. "They are right here."

"This is wrong," Shruti told herself more than she told Paridhi. "Ghosts don't roam around like that."

She got up and looked out of the window, but her reaction was quite opposite to that of Paridhi.

"They aren't ghosts," she whispered, observing the wraith-like figures moving into the alley. "They are the end of ghosts."

She took Paridhi's arm and pulled her away from the windows and dropped the curtains.

"*Enforcers*" she announced. "They haven't seen us yet, but they know that we are around here. It's just a matter of time before they find us. You have to leave."

"And what about you?" asked Sam "I am not leaving you alone."

"Sam, we don't have time for this. *enforcer*s are very selective but they prefer not to leave any witnesses. They've come for me, but if you are around when they find me, you'll both die with me."

"That doesn't mean that I will abandon you. You are my friend."

"I will be fine, I promise you," Shruti touched Sam's face to reassure him. "I won't fight them, that'd be foolish. I will run away, but you need to leave before I do. Please try and understand."

Sam shook his head despondently. He hugged Shruti for as long as he could, then took Paridhi's hand and turned to leave.

"Hey Sam," Shruti called out for him. "Take care of Paridhi all your life. Keep her safe and happy."

Sam jerked his head as he turned around and placed his glasses over his eyes. "I won't promise you anything. You'll have to come over and see to it for yourself."

"I will. You can count on me for that."

Sam gave a final nod and left. Shruti stared at the empty doorway for a while and then settled down on the bed peacefully. She had no intention of running, and she had intention of fighting either. She had lived enough. Now it was time to end all the façade. She closed her eyes and hoped that her demise would be as peaceful as the passing moment. Anasuya's words filled her mind and cleared out the last traces of doubt.

Remember, we can't run forever. We can only hope that when we die, we die after having lived. It's not about living forever. It's about creating something that does.

She had created that something. She had found a family, and she had made a family. Sam would keep her alive. A smile glowed upon her face.

The next moment an enforcer was standing right in front of her. Its towering wraith-like body seemed to block out all the light in the world. It hovered a few inches above ground too, which made it even more intimidating. Shruti sighed and tried to look into its eyes, or wherever they should've been. The *enforcer* bent its head a little to its right. Shruti felt a sudden panic grip her stomach. She had just come back to life. The *enforcer*s should've at least given her a day to get the feel of it. She shook her head.

"What now? Are you just going to stand there and stare at me?"

The *enforcer* walked away.

Shruti couldn't believe it. She just stood there and watched the other *enforcer*s follow their leader out of the room. After all these years of running and hiding, she had never expected that an enforcer would waste even a second before ripping her soul apart, let alone walk away and leave her alone.

"What the hell," she smirked to herself. "You came all the way here to just say hi?"

She sat down shaking her head in disbelief and joy. There were many unsettling discrepancies with the events she had just witnessed. Who was this friend of Sam, Ritesh? Why would someone give him a Band-of-Fate? Had the *enforcer*s somehow gone crazy? No.

"They didn't come for me."

Shruti took a few moments to let her words settle down, and then she just took off. She had to stop them.

"What are *enforcers*?" Paridhi gently turned and asked Sam.

"Keep your eyes on the road," Sam reminded her. "It is too crowded today."

"Right," she sighed. "When will you start answering my questions without me having to repeat them?"

"*Enforcers* are ghost-hunters. They find and kill ghosts, no, they destroy them."

"What? Why do they do that? Ghosts are already dead, no?"

"Well, it is necessary, in a way. You know, we wouldn't want that too many ghosts overrun our planet."

"So that's why you left your friend behind; because she is…a ghost?"

"No," Sam replied, clearly irritated. "I left her because I know that she will take care of herself. She got into all this trouble because of me anyway, so leaving her was the only option."

"Are you sure that *this* was the right time to leave her? I don't know; she didn't seem to be preparing for a run. Besides, if those things hunt ghosts, what chance does a human girl have against them?"

"Just keep driving Paridhi. Wherever she is, she is happy. That's all that matters."

"Will you say the same thing when I die?" Paridhi said.

"Shut up," Sam croaked. "Nobody's dying. Shruti is going to be fine. She promised me."

"Sam, tell me if I am wrong. I think we should've brought her with us, however dangerous it appears to be. She is your friend. I'd do that for you, or Karan, or even Nisha."

Sam's eyes were well hidden behind his glasses, but Paridhi knew how he was feeling. She wasn't forcing him to help his friend, she was just encouraging him to do what he wanted to do in the first place.

"You were the one who got jealous of her, and now you are rooting for her?" Sam smiled and shook his head "Let's take the U ahead and go and get Shruti."

"That's my boy" Paridhi kissed his cheek.

"Eyes on the road, please." Sam instructed.

Paridhi made a dash for the U-turn, but the traffic got the better of her. She had to take another route to get out of the rush that is so much a part of the city life.

"Looks like we will have to take the long cut," Sam sighed. "Luck never seems to favour me, does it?"

Sam's phone rang. He looked at the screen. It was his home's landline. He crossed his fingers and took the call.

"Hello, Sam," Shruti's voice burst out from the other end. "Where are you?"

"Hey, are you okay?" Sam asked. "What happened? We are coming back for you."

"No," Shruti shouted at him. "Whatever you do, do not come back. It's not safe for you to come back here."

"I don't care Shruti. I am coming to get you."

"You don't understand the situation Sam. If you come here, you'll get us all killed."

"What are you saying?"

"The *enforcer*s, for some reason, don't recognise me. They've come for you Sam. You are their target. If they find you, they will kill you and Paridhi too. I believe they expect the young woman next to you to be me."

Sam froze. He didn't react much, though. He couldn't gather much of what Shruti said next, but his mind tried to calculate what was going on.

"Okay, do one thing," he finally broke his silence "Take my wallet from my table. There is money and my metro-card in there. Board the metro and wait for us at Rajiv Chowk. You can get there, right?"

"Yes, I've been here for a while," Shruti said "But the *enforcer*s are headed your way. You must avoid the route where they might run into you."

"Don't worry; we've already changed our route. You will have to wait for us for about an hour. We will meet you at Gate Number 1."

"Okay, hurry up."

"So we are going to Rajiv Chowk?" Paridhi asked after Sam put his phone away.

"Yes," Sam smiled "The surprises don't seem to end today. All thanks to this little thing. This purple wrist thing."

Anomaly

Boarding a metro for the first time is generally a very happy moment for most people. And for a person who died right before the Delhi metro began and then came back to life, that moment becomes a cherished memory. Whatever Shruti felt at that moment when she entered the pink carriage of the metro wasn't just elation. It was something that no author can properly explain, something that no actor or director can sufficiently express or present. It's one of those feelings that you can only estimate, both in terms of nature and magnitude. Perhaps you will take the memory of what you felt when you first jumped into a pool to swim or when you first saw your new born sister, and you'll multiply it with ten (or five, if you are an emotionally gifted female). It will be a rough idea, but you can never know how some things feel.

Shruti let her senses get a grip of the urban, almost exotic atmosphere that covered the premises of train as well as all other manifests of the DMRC. It felt sudden, as if the entire station and the tracks and the train had been plucked off of Manhattan and planted on Delhi soil. She breathed the conditioned air as if it had been imported from Mount Everest, and let her newly attained skin get the feel of the state-of-the-art interiors of the train; the seats, the poles, the hand-rests, everything. By the time she settled down, she had already reached Rajiv Chowk.

She got off and stayed near the stairs at the exit, impatiently waiting for Sam and Paridhi. They said they would reach there in an hour. She didn't get bored, though. Being alive after so long was a gift after all. She enjoyed it when the sun burnt her skin, and she loved it when the wind played with her hair. And then it started to rain, and Shruti let the drops drench her till she got cold. Living happily is a recommended course-of-action; not everybody gets to enjoy the little things that life has to offer, seven years after death. Shruti thought about the ever increasing number of people who commit suicide for petty reasons, and cursed them under her breath for being the idiots they are. Hell, our ancestors didn't have Facebook to tell them about the sheer importance of life via endless posts from various users and pages, but they knew how to face life. Who cares, though? People who kill themselves will become ghosts and learn their lesson.

"There she is," Sam tugged at Paridhi and hurried towards the station exit.

"Shruti," they called out.

Shruti turned to face them, heaved a sigh of relief, and hugged them both. "I am glad to see you two together," she said. "You look lovely."

"Yeah, we'll have the mushy talks later," Sam intervened. "You were telling me something? The *enforcer*s came for me?"

"What?"

Paridhi's reaction was quite expected, but Sam held her hand reassuringly. "It's okay dear," he said. "We'll be fine."

"Yes," Shruti said. "I hadn't expected this at all. The *enforcer*s saw me back at your place, but they did nothing. That aroused my suspicion. Why would they come to your house if they weren't looking for me? The only logical possibility is that you are the target."

"How is this possible?"

"I think it's because of this," Shruti flashed the purple wristband at Sam.

"What is this thing anyway?" Sam grew restless. "I can't understand anything at all."

"Sam, this is a Band-of-Fate. Anasuya told me about relics like this one. The Bands-of-Fate are inexhaustible sources of power used by Archangels. They have the power to alter the very course of nature. That's why they are called Bands-of-Fate."

Sam stared at her for a few moments before breaking his silence.

"This is too weird. How can such a powerful thing end up in a pile of Ritesh's wedding gifts? And if this thing is what you think it is, why are the *enforcers* after me? If they want it returned to the owner, I'd have no problems at all."

"No, they haven't come to take it. The *enforcers* are assassins. Their job is to destroy souls, and they don't do any other jobs."

"So why are they after me?"

"At this point, all I have is speculation. This Band-of-Fate brought me back to life when I was supposed to be destroyed. That was my fate and this thing changed it. But we accessed it together, and now the *enforcers* are after you instead of me. I think that this band somehow exchanged your fate with mine."

Paridhi gasped in horror and put a hand to her mouth.

"Right," Sam breathed. "So now you live in my place and I die in yours."

"I think we are both fated to die," Shruti took his hand "The Band-of-Fate tried to exchange our fates, but it is too unnatural to be done effectively."

"And what use would that be? No matter what we do, one of us has to die."

"Yes, but that was supposed to be me. Sam, I lived my life and I died. I spent seven years as a ghost. I've had enough. But look at you. Your life has just started. Look at Paridhi. She needs you. I need you to get a hold of yourself. We're going to fix this."

"Okay, but how do you suggest we do that?"

Shruti stared around for a while and shook her head.

"I don't know much," Paridhi jumped in, "but I think the first step would be to run."

"She is right" Shruti smiled. "We need to keep eluding them, and they won't make it easy."

Sam nodded and took Paridhi aside.

"Look," Sam took her arm, "this mess has nothing to do with you. Whatever this is, I will handle it. You should go home Paridhi. We will take care of it."

"Oh no," Paridhi announced, freeing her arm. "I am not leaving you. Wherever you go, I'll go with you."

"Don't be stubborn," he said. "This could be dangerous. It's life and death at stake here."

"Do I look like I care?"

"Let her come," Shruti put a hand on Sam's shoulder. "The *enforcers* don't hurt people they have no business with. I thought they would just kill everything they encounter but a recent experience has made me wiser."

"See? She agrees with me."

Sam looked at Paridhi for a good long minute before answering. "Fine, you can come."

"Check the house."

"Acknowledged; proceeding to analyse."

117 glided over the surface of the ground as he made his way into the house.

"Be careful," 12 instructed. "Don't engage any humans you find, even if they approach you with hostility. Just observe and leave."

117 grew a little uneasy. Although most enforcers were created devoid of any real emotions, some of them still had some trivial hunches that could be compared to human emotions. Not much, just little things like intuition, surprise, uneasiness, at the most. 117 thought that they had been deliberately programmed into them to make them more effective.

'Thought' 117 shook his cloaked head. 'What a human choice of words.' Enforcers didn't think. They just analysed and concluded. 'I should be careful with my words.'

"Hey, are you there?"

"Yes, 12," 117 replied. "I understand; entering the premises now."

"Acknowledged, 117"

117 entered the house through the main door because the walls appeared to be enchanted with powerful antagonistic spells. He approached with stealth; although humans can't see enforcers, but they don't enchant their walls either. Besides, getting direct orders from Squad 13 meant that the mission was top priority. He had been informed that the Purple Dai had been located 242 sectors southwest of his location, but the ineffective Squad 2 had been given the task to find it and retrieve it. This could only mean that either the High Archangel had lost his mind, or whatever 117 was about to encounter was a lot more important than even the Purple Dai.

117 saw a young human female appear in the corridor. He took utmost care not to appear in its line of sight, even though he was most probably invisible to it. *The human was dressed in a white coat and formals, suggesting that it must've been a Healer of the human community. They used a very funny term for their healers. 'Doctor', a word that had always been used to imply adulteration, and the humans used it to speak of the noblest creatures of their race. Meanwhile, the 'Doctor' took a gulp of an orange coloured juice and tiptoed carelessly. It appeared to be in some hurry, so it left without looking around.*

'Nothing out of the ordinary here,' 117 concluded, 'But I must search the entire house.'

He retraced the human female's steps and made his way to the end of the corridor. He didn't realize that it was visible from the room, though.

"What the hell?"

A sudden male voice threw 117 off guard, and he forgot his instructions for a moment and unsheathed his Scythe. He couldn't swing it, though, as a strong wave of energy hit him and jerked the Scythe off of his grasp. Another wave of energy pinned 117 to the wall.

"I see that you are stronger than the rest of your kind, enforcer," the voice taunted him.

"I am no ordinary enforcer," 117 gasped. "Leave me alone."

"Oh, I don't know and I certainly don't care," the man quipped. "I didn't wander into your house and point a weapon at your ass."

"I didn't do it on purpose. You surprised me."

The heavy concurrence of energy eased away, and 117 slowly got up. A slight impulse of awe travelled through him as he saw the man standing in front of him. It was a human, but it wielded immense power.

"You...you are..." 117 was short of words.

"Yes, but didn't you know that already?"

"No, actually I didn't. I was sent here just to observe and leave quietly."

"Wait a second," the human looked confused. "Who sent you?"

"I was sent by the High Archangel."

The human seemed to ponder over his words for a long time. Finally, it shook its head and asked him to leave. "Right, get your butt out of my place. Next time I won't spare you if I catch you spying around here."

117 hovered away and left the house. As soon as he was clear of the place, 12's voice appeared in his mind.

"117, come in," she pinged forcefully. "Report status!"

"I am fine," he replied. "The house was enchanted. I lost you in there but I didn't get spotted. And I think I found what you were looking for."

"Go ahead, 117. Tell me everything."

He gave her a full report of whatever he had seen inside, except for the fact that the human had almost captured him. 12 thanked him and ordered him to keep observing the humans until the next order, and signed off.

"Give me good news, 12."

The voice belonged to the Second Lieutenant and it was unmistakable. She approached 12 as soon as she ended the transmission.

"You were right, Second Lieutenant," she handed him a file. "Ritesh Chahal has not received it. The plan has been going smoothly so far."

"Good work, 12. The Second Lieutenant wants to finish this case himself. On top of that, we have two stupid nomad excuses for immortals who were covering the enemy's tracks all this time. But we won't let that stop."

"Now that we have proof of the fact that this human is in fact safe, it's only obvious that Squad 10 raised a false alarm. They must have known the truth all this time."

"I know that," growled Second Lieutenant. "But we are going to leave it at that for now. I am pretty sure that Squad 10 struck a deal with the immortals in exchange of keeping the human away from our attention. I think those two immortals promised to help Squad 10 with some ancient ghost."

"You sound so sure of yourself, I could swear that you made the whole thing happen."

"Too bad 12," Second Lieutenant smiled. "Your smartness never ceases to amaze me."

There was a deafening explosion in the Communications tower of Squad 13 headquarters. The entire tower was nearly consumed in flames. The group of enforcers working on the firefighting were sure that nobody could make it out of the tower. But they had forgotten that their Second Lieutenant was one of the oldest and strongest Second Lieutenants the enforcer squads had ever served under. Hence, the surprise wasn't long-lived when Second Lieutenant appeared out of the flames, hurt, but unharmed. There weren't any other survivors.

"What happened, Second Lieutenant?" The enforcers asked her. "How did this fire come up?"

"It was 12," said Second Lieutenant. "She brought an accountant into the tower without prior information or safety protocols. Saurush, I think, was his name. This was not an accident. This was a targeted attack."

"A lot of our squad members crossed over, thanks to this. This is really bad, Second Lieutenant. Our squad has been depleted gravely in this accident."

"That's not the sum of all our problems. 12 discovered shortly before her passing away that one of the members of the squad had been turned. She found out that he had been selling information to the enemies. I think that maybe what happened to 12 and the rest of our communications team was planned out by this mole."

"Who is it, Second Lieutenant?" The speaker, number 7 of Squad 11 unsheathed his scythe and roared. "He will pass on before he reaches here."

"The traitor, as Twelve found out, is 117 of our squad. I'd suggest you go and finish him off yourself. But I'll also advise you to do it quickly and quietly, and not talk to 117 as well."

"I know very well, Second Lieutenant," said 7. "He will be dealt with right now. I'll bring my tracker and leave immediately."

Second Lieutenant smiled maliciously as she watched 7 load his weapon and leave. 7 was a ruthless killing machine of the 10th squad, also known as the Punishment Force. The squad killed first and asked questions later, because they were primarily handed out tasks based on predetermined judgements done by the other squads. By sending 7, Second Lieutenant had ensured that 117 would be reaped before he could create any problems for Second Lieutenant's plans. It was time to move on to the next phase of the plot.

Paridhi was an excellent driver, and not only by the standards of a girl. She had managed to maintain a good speed on one of the busiest road networks of the country. Of course, that meant jumping a few red-lights and defying the speed limit as well, but it's better to die in a car accident and become a ghost than to get your soul ripped and annihilated by some freakish androids of nature.

"Why am I sitting in the back?" Sam complained.

"It is safer that you sit there," Paridhi replied.

"Well," Sam smirked. "I have the equipment to see the *enforcer*s, not you."

Shruti turned to face him, and she had a meaner smirk. "Well," she said softly. "You are the one they are hunting, not her."

Sam just stared. "Why do I even try to argue with girls?"

Shruti laughed at his comment, shaking her head. "Finally, you are learning."

They went off the road soon, and Sam had no idea where they were. He had never seen this part of Delhi, and he wondered if they were in Delhi at all.

"What is this place?"

"This is somewhere near Gurgaon," Shruti answered.

"What? This is impossible! We were well inside Delhi a few minutes ago. How did we reach here so fast?"

"Let's just say I created a little shortcut."

"You *created* a shortcut?"

"Yeah, a little spatial anomaly is not a big issue. I came back to life, but I'll always be a ghost. And this wrist-band provides me with a lot of energy, seemingly inexhaustible."

"Oh my God," Paridhi chuckled. "I am living the dream here. Ghosts, ghost hunters, spatial anomalies, infinite power sources, it's like we are in a movie. Sam, you should've told me about her before."

"Well, it's never too late," Sam muttered. "You remember Nisha's accident? Well, it wasn't an accident. It was Shruti."

"What; really?"

"Not exactly," Shruti hopped in. "If you remember it properly; I did possess her for a while, but it was you who pushed her off."

"Oh, shit," Paridhi laughed. "So Karan was right after all. You pushed her off."

"Okay, that's enough. We have a live or die situation here. We can save these discussions for later, if that ever comes."

"Yes, you are right. We got to speed up now. I can sense…"

She never got to complete her sentence. A violent crash sent their car rolling across the ground. an enforcer had tracked them and fired some sort of cannon-type weapon. Shruti had managed to protect them from a direct impact, but the car couldn't hold ground against such power. Sam was shaking, all bloodied and battered. Paridhi was completely knocked unconscious and Shruti didn't look too good either. Sam held her hand, still reeling under the shock. Shruti mouthed an inaudible 'it is okay' and smiled at him, but she didn't have any strength left.

Dying like this was better than becoming a ghost anyway, at least that's what he told himself to accept what was to come. A funny feeling made him smile back, because he realized that he hadn't yet seen an enforcer. And he never would. His eyes closed on him, so did the curtains…

207 smiled as he slashed at the red car with his scythe. He was the best shot in his squad and the ablest tracker as well. But finding the humans with the Purple Dai 32 sectors south-west of their last recorded location was a coincidence that he had never expected.

"Did you get them, 207?" 13 had the habit of talking all the time to keep track of every move the squad made. Though it was an effective strategy, 207 preferred keeping things quiet. So the incessant pings made him uneasy.

"I hit them, but it seems that they manifested an energy field which took the brunt of the charge. The vehicle has been rendered ineffective, though. It would be easy to finish them off."

"Be careful 207," 13 said. *"According to the database, the ghost who turned human again, recently, on board is a seven-year old. It cannot manifest fields that can stop a scythe's charge. I am sure it used the Purple Dai to do it."*

"Gratitude for the update, 13. But I think I took them by surprise. I don't expect them to put up much of a fight. I'll check with you when I'm done."

"Affirmative", said 13.

207 pulled out his Scythe. Despite his confidence about the humans and the ghost being vulnerable, he heeded 13's advice and proceeded with caution. Still, he was sure that the ghost wasn't much of a threat. If the ghost would've been considered dangerous, Squad 1 would never have got the task of reaping the human accompanying her.

"Nearly there," 207 said as he hovered towards the wrecked car. *"Approaching the vehicle."*

He made sure that his Scythe was always ahead of him and ready. He had always been a cautious camper. He grabbed the frame of a door and broke it off the car. Slowly, he sat down to observe the contents.

"Funny," he pinged. *"It seems that we underestimated the ghost."*

13 was still working on her next question when echoes of an explosion overwhelmed all the lines of communications. A near stampede broke out in the office as enforcers rushed to protect the little equipment that had survived.

"This is bad," 13 sighed. *"They got away!"*

Sam's eyes opened to a sense of motion. He could feel landscapes passing him by, but it felt very serene. He felt as if he was lying on a grass bed which was hitched to a ride. Slowly, his eyes adjusted to the light, and he could see Paridhi's face. The constant revving of an engine blocked out her starting few words, but he picked on.

"…awake. You lazy boy, you've been sleeping in my lap for hours now."

Sam got up, shaking his head. He caught a glimpse of green fields of sugarcane stretching as far as the horizon went. Paridhi caressed his hair, kissed his cheek and rubbed her face against his face lovingly.

"Oh baby," she breathed softly. "You're okay now!"

Sam smiled and hugged her lightly. He realized that they were in a big truck zooming across some highway. Shruti was driving.

"Where are we?"

"We are in a truck," Shruti grimaced. "I can't tell you any more than that, or we will land in a bigger truck."

"What are you trying to say?"

"Nothing, I was just trying some pun. The second time, the word 'truck' meant chaos."

"Now she talks like you," Paridhi quipped. "Genius logic, out of the blue, and nobody gets the joke."

"We were in a car," Sam asked. "We got hit. What happened?"

Shruti grinned ear to ear at his question.

"Somebody please explain this to me. What happened?"

"Well," Shruti spoke with elegance. "The *enforcers* did what I had expected them to do. And I used the most common trick that ghosts employ to evade them."

"What did you do, then?"

"You remember spatial anomalies? That did the trick."

"I am looking forward to an elaborate answer."

"Well, I told you that we were in Gurgaon. I lied. Our car was in Gurgaon but we weren't. We never left Delhi. Until the *enforcers* attacked, that is."

Sam gaped at her in utter disbelief.

"Goddamn it," he whispered. "You...you...saved me."

"Yeah," Shruti sounded almost indifferent. "You sort of gave me a new life, and I am not talking about the literal second life I got because of you. You are my best friend, so I owe you a lot more than one near-death experience."

"We are safe, I can't believe it."

"Yes, but they are still looking for us. So we could use our present status. I died seven years ago, and the two of you went missing three hours back."

"I slept for three hours? That means we shouldn't be far from Delhi."

"No, you were unconscious for three hours. And yes, we shouldn't be far from Delhi, but we are. Don't forget about the spatial anomalies. I have a way with them."

Sam smiled and relapsed into the seat. The landscape kept passing them by, but it still stayed with them. The vast sugarcane fields, the rising sun to the left, and the canals that came at almost regular intervals.

"It's too bad for my mom," he said. "She will be worried, or just sad. Karan and Nisha will miss us as well. I guess the end isn't so nice from their perspective."

"I don't know," Shruti said. "People always seem to find out happiness in life. Especially people close to bright and radiant personalities like you two. Besides, it's far from over as of yet. You chose to haunt a ghost, now you're going to have a lot on your plate to deal with."

Epilogue

Ritesh juggled with the glass in his hand as he opened the bottle of Scotch yet again. He filled his glass the third time and gulped it down in one ruthless go.

"I thought you had quit?"

The voice didn't invoke any reaction from Ritesh. He just filled his glass again, and downed another peg.

"I am too pissed off to care about any promises or resolves right now."

"That's why you are seeking solace in alcohol," the voice seemed to prick him. "Such a Piscean move."

"I am not in the mood for fooling around," Ritesh growled.

"Neither am I. I came here to tell you something very important."

"Nothing is important to me right now, rather than…"

"Rather than figuring out a way to save your wife, isn't it?"

Ritesh's inebriation was washed away instantly. He staggered up to his feet and looked around quizzically.

"What did you find out?"

"I found out that your friend can save your wife."

"But Samved has been missing for three months. Isn't he dead?"

"Oh, he is alive. But it's only a matter of time before the enforcers find him and take him out."

"Not if I find him first." The voice seemed to linger too long. "What happened?"

"You'll have to kill him."

Ritesh froze. His eyes blinked rapidly for a while and then closed up. "Are you out of your fucking mind?"

"You knew this already Ritesh," the man said. "You knew this all the time, and now you are trying to deny it."

"I can't do this," he screamed.

"Either you will do this, or the enforcers will. Samved dies either way. The question is whether his death saves Radhika or not."

Ritesh didn't answer. He knew that his guide had left. He just sat back, poured another glass, and gulped it down.

"Damn it Sam," he grunted. "Why did you have to steal from me?"